PECK FINCH AND THE HANGED MAN

A Peck Finch Novel

Jerome Mark Antil

"Promise of Liberty lacks measure to the despondent. Until we care enough there will never be a free America. We must curb the pallor of desperation—the stem of human trafficking. Until basic food and shelter are a fundamental right in defining freedom—there will always be slaves in America. Freedom of speech is mute when one has no voice."

JMA

LITTLE YORK
BOOKS
New York · NY · Dallas · TX

1.

IT WAS JUST AFTER MIDNIGHT when Peck found a space around the corner from the law office and parked. The elevator to the second-and third-floor offices was locked after hours so he climbed three flights of stairs and let himself in.

His usual routine was a shout-out of his name so he wouldn't alarm anyone who might be working late. Switching on the third-floor lights, his next routine, if it wasn't raining, was a jaunt down to the dark second floor to open Lily Cup's window to air out her cigar smoke. Then it was back up to the third floor, scrubbing the coffee room, the bathroom and bowls, dusting baseboards and emptying wastebaskets. Finishing the third floor, he turned the lights off and stepped down to the dark second floor.

Reaching for the light switch was when he heard the scream.

He left the lights off and followed the street sounds in the dark and made it through the front rooms to Lily Cup's office window. He cautiously stood back, watching Carrolton Avenue below. A white man wearing a brown fedora with a heavy gold-chained band and a double-breasted black sport coat stood between two white girls. A black Mercedes was parked in idle with its lights on. One girl was leaning on the driver's seat of a pedicab. The man was gripping the upper arm of the girl standing on the sidewalk.

"Whatchu' doin' over here? Why ain't you workin'? Why you peddling around with this bitch?" He back-handed her jaw. The girl muffled a scream and lost her balance.

Peck knew if he shouted, he could trigger deadly violence, but his primal instincts kicked in, and he knew if he didn't shout out, he might be able to track this bad man.

"Don't hurt her," the girl on the pedicab shouted. "She's got a job with me. It's a real job. Why can't you just leave her alone?"

The man pulled a polished stainless steel .45 caliber semiautomatic from his back belt, cocked it and pointed it at the pedicab girl's face.

"Cuz I'm her real job, bitch"— he touched the point of the gun to her forehead—"and this here's my boss."

"No," the girl on the sidewalk begged. "Don't do it. I'll go with you."

"What you say, bitch?" the man asked the pedicab girl. "You want to piss my boss here off, or you gonna' mind yo' own fuggn' bizness and pedal yo' ass on out of heya?"

"I'll go," the girl begged. She tried to start pedaling. The man put his foot on the tire, impeding its movement.

"Cuz of you my lady ain't earned me nuthin' tonight. Who's gonna pay?"

"Don't shoot. Please."

"Who's gonna' pay, bitch? My boss ain't happy. See? He's getting twitchy."

"Take my money. Take it."

With the gun hand he unzipped her purse and pulled out the cash. He threw the purse into her pedicab and flipped the gun, lowering his leg and motioning her to take off.

Shaking and in tears, the girl stood and pedaled a U-turn and headed toward the French Quarter without looking back. The man stood motionless, watching her pedal out of sight. He slipped the pistol under his belt, clenched his fist and slugged the girl in the stomach, doubling her over. She fell to her knees gasping.

"Don't you ever disrespect me."

He kicked her. He leaned and grabbed her hair, lifted her head and stuck his face into hers.

"Don't I feed you good?"

"Yes."

"Don't I give you a bed? Don't I buy you pretty things?"

"I'm sorry. Really, I'm sorry."

He pulled the revolver from his belt and pressed it to her ear.

"You step out of Storyville without permission again and your little sister in that foster home up in Georgia ain't never g'wan to see 'nudder day. I know where she lives. Understand?"

"Fire ant," Peck said to himself.

Peck carefully pushed the window closed without a slam, and with instincts he learned on a pirogue in a swamp filled with deadly alligators he made a dash to the stairwell and jumped down two steps at a time, repeating a quiet cadence of guttural sounds all the way down.

He reached his pickup, started it with the lights off and crept to the corner. In idle he watched with the patience of a crawfish snake waiting for its prey to come by.

"C'mon fire ant … show Peck your mound."

Peck watched the man yank the girl to her feet and push her into the back seat. He memorized the license plate. The man removed his hat, showing a diamond stud in his left ear and a two-inch bright red tattoo of a dollar sign on his neck. He got in the back seat and the car sped off. Peck began following as if he was in a swamp, tracking a gator. He didn't have revenge in his eyes; he was tracking for a future hunt, but he was likely remembering being abused as a young boy, slaved and chained under a porch by the gator man. He likely remembered Lily Cup's talking about how the pimps always seemed to get off in court because of legal technicalities or bad copping, or by no one knowing their secret hideouts. Peck wouldn't take anyone down that night, but he had a long memory. All he wanted that night was an address.

He followed the car into Storyville. It came to a stop idling with lights on. Without slowing he drove past it. Through his rearview mirror he could see the man and girl walk toward a three-story townhome with a boarded-up storefront on its first floor. Peck turned right, pushed his headlights off, and made a quick U-turn and waited at the corner. The man had sunglasses on, and diamonds were in both ears. He couldn't see the man's face clearly, but he could see the tattoo and he saw a reflection off the girl's nose ring.

The Mercedes drove off and turned left on Basin Street.

"The mound," Peck said to himself, memorizing the street address. He followed the car, keeping a distance. After various turns, it entered a parking garage of a trendy high-rise hotel on Canal Street.

Peck passed by and drove back to the law offices. He finished cleaning and went home to his bedroom, where he lived with Gabe in a classic shotgun in the Garden District. Stacks of books in his bedroom were monument to his phoenix from illiteracy. A reading lamp on the floor in the corner lighted his favorite place to lie on his side and read his books. When Millie wasn't in town, he'd sleep alone but next to the bed on the floor under an open window, looking up at the moon for hours. He picked up his John Steinbeck novel from his desk and sat on the floor, thinking. He looked up through the window blinds. There was a full moon that night and Peck had a lot on his mind.

2.

HAVING BEEN SLAVED IN A BAYOU SWAMP in his early childhood, Cajun French Peck knew what it was like to be alone, with no one to turn to. His only go-to support between the age of five and an illiterate young adulthood was his imagination of full moons, with his mamma looking back at him and his discovery of the Mass, after learning the Christ child grew up to hang on a cross. It was still dark when Peck got up off his bedroom floor and went to Gabe's bedroom.

"You awake, Gabe?" Peck asked.

He nudged the bedroom door ajar.

"Captain, I need to talk. I made some chicory."

Gabe, a retired army captain who had served with distinction in both Korea and Vietnam, yawned, pushed himself up to a sitting position, then stepped over to his easy chair in the living room and waited.

Peck came in and handed Gabe a mug of chicory.

"Captain, I couldn't talk about this until I give it thinking time," Peck said.

"My brother. Whatever it is, I'm here for you. What time is it?"

"It's five in the morning, ol' man. Sorry."

Peck sat, sipped and swallowed while gazing at the framed picture of Gabe's dead son in uniform on the mantle. Peck watched Gabe's eyes.

"Gabe, you remember about me being slaved when I was at Bayou Chene?"

"I remember," Gabe said. "You were a child."

"Gabe, you knew gator man who slaved me. He got killed by a man from Angola prison, right?"

"I'm sworn not to speak of it, my brother, but yes, I've heard the story."

"Gabe did you know my own daddy was shot when he tried to kill Dr. Pontelbon in that fishing boat?"

"Peck, let's not dredge up these memories, we have a good life now. Just look at you— we're all so proud."

"Did you know, Gabe? About Daddy bein' shot like that?"

"The man fathered you by raping your mother, son. He was never your daddy. He deserved to be shot."

Peck stared at the ottoman and reflected.

"Gabe, last night I watched a man slave a girl."

"What do you mean?"

"This girl, Gabe. She couldn't be maybe twelve or fourteen— was on Carrollton Avenue. He beat her and took her away with a gun."

"He kidnapped her?"

"He said she was his whore and he slugged her hard."

"I'm sorry you had to see that, Peck."

"Gabe, it was good I saw it, I say."

"Good? Why?"

"You teach me to always pay back, Gabe."

"I do teach that, son."

"Gabe, I have to help that girl."

Gabe sat up in his recliner, accidently splashing coffee on an arm of the chair. Peck pulled his T-shirt off over his head and tossed it to use as a towel.

"Help?" Gabe asked.

"*Oui.*" ("Yes.")

With seasoned military eyes Gabe stared at Peck.

"And you'll do anything to save her?"

Peck didn't respond.

"With all you've gone through, Peck, a dirt poor Cajun French kid on your own since you can remember. You're white but you understand and know poverty—maybe you can imagine what being black is like in America—"

"Nah-nah, Gabe. Not even close to what you been through, my black frien'. I'm sorry."

"What it feels like knowing white eyes objectify you as a thief or a crack head, a worthless parent?"

"Ah *oui.*"

"Well son, sex predators objectify kids the same way. Boys, girls, they don't care, they look at them as pieces of meat."

"Is that what *objectify* means, Gabe?"

"That's what it means, son. Looking through a human as if they're a toy or a tool or worse—a nobody."

Peck stood, took Gabe's coffee cup and the coffee-blotched T-shirt, and stepped out of the room. He reentered wearing a fresh T-shirt and with a cup of coffee in his hand for Gabe.

"Will you listen to some advice, son?"

"*Oui.*"

"I know how serious you are about this, Peck, and as smart as you are, I have a feeling you'll succeed in getting this girl out of the mess she's in."

"I will, dass for true, Gabe."

"I just have one suggestion."

"Okay."

"It's an important one, son."

"Okay."

"Before you do anything, have a talk with Lily Cup. She knows this world you saw last night. It's the world she lives in and works in every day."

Peck nodded. He leaned in like he wanted to whisper.

"Secret question, okay, Gabe?"

Gabe lowered his head and looked over the tops of his reading glasses at Peck and rolled his eyes—as if Peck knew better than to ask if he could count on Gabe's secrecy.

"Somebody kidnaps a little girl to sell for sex, would you conk him, the one what steals the girl to sell for sex or would you conk the money what buys the girl for sex?"

Gabe lifted his coffee.

"Sex slavery is a dangerous game, son."

"How, Gabe?"

"There's a lot of money in it. Big money."

"Okay."

"Did you actually see them kidnap her, or were they catching her not working the streets?"

"She was running."

"You mean she was running away from a pimp?"

"Ah *oui*. The pimp he said she worked Storyville, but he found her on Carrollton, trying to run away."

"She'll never get away from them. They'd just as soon snuff her as look at her before they'd let her set a bad example for the others by escaping."

"Snuff?"

"Kill."

"I'm goin' to get her out."

Gabe studied the gray of conviction in Peck's eyes.

"You remember my stories, son? My army days in Kentucky when buddies and I caught buses into Newport and went to those second-floor whorehouses?"

"Ah, *oui*. I remember."

"Those whorehouses were run by the mob, Peck. We thought it was exciting, a normal part of life in the big city. Every man jack of us thought those women did it because they liked sex. It never entered our mind they were slaves and couldn't leave those beds even if they wanted to. They probably all died in their twenties or thirties from syphilis or some other VD."

"Ah-yee," Peck said.

"Every time me and the fellas put up our twelve dollars for a roll on the sheets with one of them, we were giving the mob reason to enslave more girls. Me and my army buddies were financing sex slavery. We were the traffickers in those days, son. We just didn't know any better at the time."

Peck didn't respond.

"I spent a lot of time in 'Nam and Seoul, South Korea and saw it big time. Sex slavery preys on poverty. I heard about parents selling their kids off for cash."

"This girl needs my help, Gabe."

"You need me for anything, son— you come to me."

"Gabe I've got to read some and then get ready."

"But you'll talk to Lily Cup first?"

"*Oui*."

"How about we do Charlie's tonight. The ladies will be there. It'll give you a chance to talk with Lily Cup," Gabe said. "Just talk with her before you do anything."

"Okay. I'll come back and take you to Charlie's."

"Come back? Where are you off to now, son?"

"Gabe, I'm going to Mass and then I go to see my mamma."

"That's a long drive Peck, are you sure—?"

"I need me some advice, Gabe. Mamma give me good advice. I need to hear about gator man again, is all."

"And you'll come back tonight, son?"

"Sun coming up, Gabe. There's a morning moon. I go to Mass, then drive to see Mamma and talk and I come back and take you to Charlie's."

"My brother. Be safe."

Peck went to his bedroom. He picked up his John Steinbeck novel and stepped over to a window and looked out. He looked at the corner of St. Charles Avenue and watched a streetcar go by. He mumbled to a world of evil he was seeing for a second time but through a new set of eyes. Then as if he was talking to the enslaved girl.

"I'm coming for you, bébé. Tell red dollar tattoo man, I'm coming for him too. He ain't going to see another full moon and dass for true."

Gabe was napping in his recliner when Peck stepped into the kitchen on his way out. Gabe heard him and raised his head.

"Gabe, after Charlie's tonight if you don't see me a few days, don't you worry, frien', I'm good. Somebody'll be lookin' in on you."

"My brother," Gabe whispered. "Just promise me you'll talk with Lily Cup before you do anything, Peck. Can you make me that promise, son?"

"I promise, Gabe. I see you tonight when I get back. We go to Charlie's."

3.

WHENEVER PECK WOULD DRIVE to visit his mamma, he'd begin the day celebrating his climb from an early youth of homelessness and illiteracy by attending morning mass at Cathedral Basilica in Jackson Square. He'd genuflect, bless himself, and before kneeling in prayer he'd light a vigil candle with a gift of thanks for his new life. The sparkle from candles and the splendor of God's house were refuge from memories of a youth in Carencro when he was a nine-year-old runaway sleeping in a trash bin at the slaughter house or on a cot in Marcel LaFleur's unheated wooden blade shed.

Teaching himself how to read, this twenty-four-year-old gentle Cajun French soul retained an Acadian patois as a part of his past, but found glory in hearing the reverence in the simple message of a Mass cloaked in symbols of majesty like were the original gifts of gold, frankincense, myrrh and now painted window glass. Colorful reflections lifted his spirits to believe there was more to this life, more than the streets and swamps. Something bigger than self. Peck believed finding his mamma after almost twenty years was a miracle. The Mass raised the bar of thought, fueling the long drive with quality think time. A good fisher is a good thinker. In his youth, Peck was a good fisher.

Following Mass, Peck was driving out of New Orleans when his phone rang. He saw it was his Millie, a senior at Baylor University. He knew it would be best to keep her from the drama.

"Hello, Millie, how you are lover girl?"

"I'm surprised you even remember my name," Millie said.

"Oh, cher, why my Millie talk to me like that?"

"I'm lonely, that's why! And I have nobody to talk to."

"*Mais non mon*— nah nah. Peck loves Millie more than anything— more than— well, anything is all. Why you so sad, cher?"

"You never answer my texts."

"Hanh?" ("*Huh?*")

"You leave me here in Waco, sleeping all alone."

"Millie, I text you back. It was 1:15 in the morning. I can see it on my phone, but then you texted me fourteen more times while I was reading my book for university and sleeping. Honest, cher, Peck had to read a big book and then I watched the moon and thought of you all night in my sleep, I promise."

"You promise?"

"I promise, cross my heart. Why so many texts?"

"I have to write a final paper."

"What paper?"

"My Civics (Civil Law) class."

"You'll do good, bébé. I love you."

"Well, alrighty then," Millie said. "I forgive you."

"Thanks Millie. I love you."

"Give Lily Cup a hug," Millie said. "Tell her I have a week coming up, and I'll let her know when. Oh, look at the time! I've got to get ready for class, love you—bye."

As his phone went blank Peck grinned. He called Bait Man Alex, his friend who lived near his mamma.

"Hello stranger," Bait Man Alex said.

"Where you at, my frien'? I'm on my way to see Mamma. What say you come make a party and toss some traps on the bank? We pass a good time. I have things to ax you too."

"How long will you be here, Peck?"

"Ah, I get there maybe three— two hour. I head back to New Or-lee-anh, say six, six-thirty, so I can take my frien' to Charlie's for jazz."

Alayna's houseboat was motorless, and it floated on an inlet by the Diversion Canal and Amite River in Acadiana. Peck would leave his pickup on the bank by the giant willow tree—the "willer," he remembered since his early childhood—before boarding. His Russian friend, Bait Man Alex, brought his wife by, and they came early, with a plastic bag filled with chicken necks and parts for Peck's crab traps and another bag with freshly caught fish they'd cook for an early supper before Peck would have to leave.

Bait Man Alex baited twenty crab traps and tossed them down the banks of the inlet ten on each side of the houseboat. As Peck drove in Bait Man Alex was grilling fish onshore on charcoal with corncobs, zucchini and bananas. It was always a warm and happy time, them being together. Peck pulled the traps while Bait Man Alex cooked. He'd pop the shells, rinse the innards and ice them.

"You maybe want cinnamon chicory, Mamma, or do you want lemonade?" Peck asked.

"Lemonade, honey, but let me get a pen so I can make notes," Mamma said. "You know my memory."

She gathered her pen, pad, pulled a chair and sat to the left of Bait Man Alex's wife, at the right of Peck and across from Alex.

"Mamma, ever'body, I'm reading a book. It's by this fella John Steinbeck. It's called *The Grapes of Wrath*, but it's not about grapes, it's about the Depression. That's the time way back when the whole country was poorer like anything and the land was dried up and all blistered and dusty and people were starving and dying along roadsides in towns they ain't never heard of or been to before."

"I remember reading that in school, Boudreau. Oh my— hearing you describe it brings it alive again."

"*The Grapes of Wrath* was a classic in Russia," Bait Man Alex said.

"I'm to the part where the boy, well he's a grown man now who did some prison time— his name is Tom Joad. See, it's late at night and that Tom Joad fella just conked a camp guard dead under the bridge. The man deserved it for killing Casy, who wasn't doing anythin' but listening to a union man, but now Tom has to run off middle of the dark, so they don't catch and hang him, and that's when his mamma ax him, 'Tom, how will I know where you are?'

And that's when Tom says, 'I'll be everywhere. Wherever you can look—wherever there's a fight so hungry people can eat, I'll be there. Wherever there's a cop beatin' up a guy, I'll be there.' It goes on like that, but it's beautiful, dass for true."

Mamma leaned and gently touched Peck's cheek.

"You have a good heart, Boudreaux Clemont. You're a good man."

"You think he was right, Mamma, Bait Man Alex? Tom Joad conking that man— think he's right?"

"To try to save a life?" Mamma asked.

"Ah *oui*, Mamma, that guard killed Casy for listening to the union man, is all. He maybe woulda' killed more."

"I think he was right, Boudreau."

"Damned right," Bait Man Alex said.

Peck sipped his chicory, lost in thought. "Mamma, did gator man ever beat on you?"

"Boudreaux, don't let that man in. Don't let that man be at this table."

"I'm sorry, Mamma."

There was a moment of silence.

"Mamma, when Mémé goes, will you be staying on the boat or will you come to New Or-lee-anh?"

Mémé had been in the insane asylum since before Peck's Mamma was born.

Mamma didn't answer.

Peck changed the subject.

"I'll bring putty next time, Mamma. Windows need spacklin'. I'll paint them too."

They finished chatting and stepped off the houseboat and over to the pickup. Peck and Bait Man shook hands.

"Thanks frien'."

"When you coming for all weekend, Peck?" Bait Man Alex asked.

"First Friday, frien'. After Mass. Soon. I promise."

Peck turned to his mamma.

"Don't forget the crabs, Mamma, they in the chest."

"You be sure to tell Gabe, Sasha and Lily Cup a hello for me, Boudreaux. Give them my love. Millie too."

"You got envelopes Mamma, anything you need you write me and I bring it First Friday sure. Promise?"

"I promise. Tell Millie thank you for her letters. They mean so much to me."

"I will Mamma."

They hugged a long goodbye.

"Mamma you need me or Bait Man Alex to light the woodstove for the crab boil?"

"It's kindled, honey, I'll be fine. You drive safe."

Alayna held a palm over her mouth and watched her only boy climb into his pickup and drive away with a warm wave through his back window.

It was a long ride home, but there was an early moon, and it was full, and Peck's mind settled by watching the moon as if he was thinking of his life. Seeing the distant New Orleans skyline sparkling like gems under a haloed crown, Peck smiled as if his mind thought of his and Gabe's friends Sasha and Lily Cup. Two successful women in New Orleans, in their late thirties. How jazz brought them together like a family. A few nights a month the affinity would call them all to dance.

The two women were best friends since they were six. One a prominent realtor, one a top criminal attorney, both never at a loss for words, a jibe, an adventure, a dry Martini. A good cigar and a tall glass of rye for Lily Cup before her murder trials. Sasha always donned the finest Givenchy, Chanel, and Louboutin the nights they'd "slut up" in their haute and head to Charlie's Blue Note in the alley just off Frenchman Street for secret nights of slow dancing to live jazz and the best red beans and rice in New Orleans. Before meeting Gabe and Peck, Charlie would walk them home.

"I get Gabe and we go to Charlie's tonight," Peck mused to himself while driving. "I talk to Lily Cup like I promised the ol' man. Maybe we dance."

He smiled while looking at oncoming headlights.

4.

GABE WAS DRESSED AND READY when Peck came home. Peck was pleased he had arrived in time. Gabe was an old man, and out of respect Peck always wanted to see to it that he'd get to Charlie's Blue Note safely any nights his friend wanted to dance jazz.

Tonight, Peck was going to get him there and have his talk with Lily Cup, as Gabe suggested. He felt good about getting Mamma's and Bait Man Alex's approval for the mission he was thinking. Maybe he'd have some beans and rice. As he and Gabe stepped from Frenchman Street into the alley toward Charlie's, the silhouette of a man appeared in the shadows. He was a tall man with nostrils exhaling animated billows of cigarette smoke as his arm reached and dropped the butt with a flick. The man snuffed it out with the toe of his burgundy lizard loafer. The man then pulled Charlie's door open and held it courteously for Gabe and Peck, almost as if he were the doorman.

Peck knew the man but didn't say anything. It was André from the Angola prison. Peck hadn't seen him for more than a year, since the time Lily Cup drove him there to listen to André tell a story of how a man ended Peck's childhood nightmares of gator man. The gator man who would chain five, six and seven-year-old Peck under his porch. The gator man who would tape Peck's mouth so he couldn't scream and drag him behind his boat as gator bait in black swamp waters.

While in prison André heard stories of what this gator man did to a young boy from Lily Cup, his criminal attorney, and André took it upon himself to orchestrate an assassination of gator man from his prison cell. André didn't know Peck at the time and Lily Cup had no knowledge of his intent. He did it as a surprise Christmas present for his favorite attorney. Lily Cup trusted Peck wouldn't talk about it—about gator man's demise and what happened or how it happened—but she wanted him to hear the story directly from André.

"Gentlemen?" André asked, holding Charlie's door.

Peck turned his head away. He remembered André served time for selling firearms, but he also remembered Lily Cup got him off murder charges.

André didn't appear to recognize Peck's face. Gabe clutched the door frame and pulled himself up the two steps into Charlie's Blue Note. Peck followed.

"Thank you," Gabe said.

"Thanks," Peck said.

"My pleasure," André said, and as if it was a coming home family reunion after being away a long time, he added, "Listen to those sounds, my friends, what beautiful sounds."

Gabe pointed at a table by the band.

"Grab our table, son," Gabe said. "I've got business." He headed to the men's room, saluting Charlie as he walked past the bar.

Peck looked for Sasha or Lily Cup, but didn't see either. André looked about, soaking everything in as if he was too long gone and wanted to refresh his memories. He sidled up to the bar, shook Charlie's hand and sat on a stool. Gabe came from the back room with eyes focusing on the band as he pulled a chair and sat while listening to a rhythm change marking a jazz finale. Peck doesn't interrupt as the saxophone hummed a slow riff of melancholy with the string bass being slapped, keeping quiet sounds alive with a pulse. Gabe's fingers outstretched and flat on the table as if he could feel vibes of drum brushes sanding a stretched hide of a snare. Gabe's eyes closed and his head rocked back and forth as if he were a blind man maneuvering through a crowded street market. The riff ended and Gabe's eyes opened. The tall blue-black sax player caught Gabe's glance with his own smiling eyes. He rested his sax on the worn leather strap around his neck and pointed a long, dark-bronze finger at Gabe, welcoming a brother home. Gabe smiled back a *thank you, my brother.*

"Any word from the ladies, Peck?" Gabe asked. "I want to dance."

Peck looked at his phone. He glanced at the bar and watched André sitting there with a drink in his hand. He was the only man at the bar in a suit.

"It's early for them," Peck said. "You want you some beans?"

Peck chose not to tell Gabe that he knew the stranger at the bar. Not yet. His gut told him the tracker in him needed to feel André out, the man who was able to personally see to it that gator man was taken care of for good while he sat behind bars miles away. Peck respected the power he yielded, and as a seasoned hunter tracker he knew he had to be careful. He had to see if this André was an opportunity for what he witnessed last night from Lily Cup's window or would André be a problem for him—a big problem? What were the odds that André was a fire ant?

"Gabe, what say we get some beans and wait for the ladies before we order drinks? If that be okay we'll wait for them."

"Good with me, my brother," Gabe said. "How about some water, no ice?"

Peck offered his fist for a pump, stood and pushed his chair in.

"I'll be back."

Sweet jazz sounds began with the bass leading a mellow parade of a foggy saxophone through velvet echoes. Gabe's eyes locked on the young man's folded knuckle as it strummed the strings of the tall bass fiddle like he was playing a harp. Peck walked to the bar, strategically leaning on it beside the empty stool next to André.

"Charlie, how you all are, frien'?" Peck asked.

Charlie turned his way.

"Everything good by me, bébé. Where you at?"

"Can I ax you mamma for some of them sweet beans and rice?"

"You know how we did it, bébé, nothing's changed," Charlie said. "This ain't no Waldorf."

"You heard from the ladies, Charlie?"

"Not since Thursday. They be in later. What can I get you boys?"

"We gonna' do water 'til the ladies come, s'okay?"

"Okay by me, order your bowls—I'll have water waiting. Ice?"

"Nah nah, no ice."

"No problem," Charlie said.

"Thanks, Charlie."

When Charlie turned away Peck cautiously poked André's arm twice with a firm finger. André turned his way.

"You remember me, frien'?" Peck asked.

André smiled.

"From the door? I remember you."

"Nah nah, before that … way before."

André looked inquisitively at Peck's eyes. "You're going to have to help me, son."

"Can we talk— back room be best, I think. Can you talk now?" Peck asked.

André looked over Peck's shoulder into the dark back room. He shrugged and nodded, stood up and followed Peck into the room and to the kitchen order window.

Peck had an anxious look, as if he'd only have one chance to keep this powerful man's attention. He readied, turned and looked eye to eye. He whispered in André's ear.

"Your name is André, and Lily Cup took me to meet you up at Angola, and that's when you told me about that bad gator man and what happened to him—the chomp, chomp, remember?"

"I'm listening," André said.

"I never forget the story you tol', Mr. André, about that bad gator man 'accidently' falling out of a pirogue in that dark bayou swamp by the cypress and gettin' eaten by alligators not far from the same porch where that gator man chain me …"

"Now I remember." André offered his hand. "Good to see you again, bébé." Peck shook André's hand, and with his other hand he embraced it.

"Can I ax you somethin', Mr. André? And maybe you goin' to tell Peck to go away and I promise you I'll go away for true, but maybe you say what I ax is okay?"

"You're Lily Cup's friend," André said. "Ask."

Through the order window Peck caught Charlie's mother's eye in the kitchen. He raised two fingers, indicating two bowls of red beans and rice. He then placed his palm on André's chest and nudged him away from the order window and into the shadows of a dark wall out of sight of the bar and order window.

"I don't know this bayou," Peck started, "but I know enough not to talk about some things and how you say—to elude other things— to be safe?"

In the dark André took Peck's hand and lifted it from his chest.

"Best get a load off your shoulders, son. Whatever's on your mind? You can talk to André."

"About anything?" Peck asked.

"Anything," André said. "Words don't cost."

"The story you tol' me about what happened to gator man—ever since you tol' me I think of you as kind of like bein' a Godfather to me, you doin' that and setting me free from nightmares I had, and dass for true, if you catch my meaning."

André stood tall with chest out. He blessed himself with a deliberate sign of the cross. He appeared genuinely honored by the sentiment.

"What I mean to say is if I ax you something now and you don't like what I ax you just say go away Peck and I go away, how you say, out of respect and I forget ever'thing I'm thinkin'. Okay, Godfather?"

André was silent. He was experienced in facial tells and he was wary enough to reflect before acting, but his face appeared to respect Peck's approach as sincere. Peck having been endorsed by Lily Cup may have gone a long way in his wanting to trust Peck. He offered his hand. Peck shook it warmly.

"André, last night I saw something, and I have to help somebody, but it's got to do with what I heard Lily Cup call trafficking. It's a bad thing, sex slavery and dass for true, but when I saw you I get an idea that I got to ax you for permission or help maybe, but first I should ax if you okay with that trafficking business and maybe you tell Peck here to go away."

With a firm grasp André took Peck by the arm and forcibly walked him back over to the light of the order window, where two bowls had just been placed on the shelf. He looked in Peck's eyes as if he was looking at his soul.

"You listen to André real good, son."

"I promise, André," Peck said.

"André has eight precious little ones at home. Well, one is attending Xavier, and one is married and in Baton Rouge with two of her own, but they're all still little ones to me. André may do some things my mamma don't approve of, but playing on poverty or innocence or with young people's lives like those devil crab animals do is not one of them. Tell me how can André help you, bébé."

Peck lifted André's hand and kissed it.

"*Merci mon ami. Merci beaucoup*," Peck said. ("Thank you, my friend. Thank you very much.")

"It's coming back to me," André started. "You're the tracker. You tracked a drug thief, that road pirate—what was it—three, maybe four, five states, and you caught him? André remembers now."

"Dass for true," Peck whispered. "Kentucky, I tied him to his refrigerator with fishing line."

André smiled. "Ah yes, the black fishing line. That fishing line was good for more than one problem, eh bébé?"

Peck knew gator man was killed in a bayou swamp with the use of black fishing line.

He smiled.

André lifted a business card from his vest pocket and handed it to Peck.

"Don't lose this."

"I won't, Mr. André."

André pointed at the bowls on the serving shelf.

"Enjoy your beans and rice. Listen to beautiful jazz, meet pretty ladies, and dance. Music and dance blend memories, don't you think, my friend? And good memories mend our souls."

"Ah *oui*," Peck said. "Thanks, Mr. André."

"Tonight, you dance, bébé."

"Ah *oui*."

"Tomorrow you track."

"Ah *oui*."

"You know to call André when you're ready."

André turned and started toward the bar.

"Thanks, my Godfather frien'," Peck said. André was out of earshot.

Peck delivered the bowls, spoons, napkins.

"Who was that?" Gabe asked.

"A man I met."

Peck spooned beans with a telling look in his eyes … it was a conflicted look, as if he was wrestling with whether or not to tell Gabe it was André. Sasha and Lily Cup approached out of nowhere. Sasha was ready to dance in a stunning strapless red satin dress, sheer black French stockings and garter belt, Louboutin heels, and a celebrated cleavage pouting on a shelf of priceless black lace ribbon. Lily Cup was in her black satin tights, leather ankle boots with bridle straps and spiked heels, wearing a black, silver-speckled French T-shirt.

"Will you just look at this pulchritude, Peck?" Gabe asked. He stood and pulled chairs. "Can you imagine heaven visiting our table tonight, my brother? Look at these two angels."

Peck stood.

"I came to dance," Lily Cup said. "But looking at the bar, I might have to work."

"André?" Peck whispered.

"André," Lily Cup said.

"Now, now, you two," Sasha said. "Work is money."

Sasha set her martini down on the table.

"Hello boys," Sasha said.

"I can't stay," Lily Cup said.

Peck leaned to Lily Cup's ear. "Can we talk?"

"Sure, call me tomorrow."

Peck raised his brow.

"You mean now?" Lily Cup asked.

"*Oui*. Gabe say we need to talk."

Over time she learned to respect Peck's instinct for urgency … and Gabe's wisdom. Both instincts were keener than anybody she had ever known.

"I saw you talking to André. Is this about him?" Lily Cup asked. She turned her head and looked in his eyes for a read.

"Nah nah," Peck said.

"It's serious, isn't it?" Lily Cup asked.

Peck nodded.

The jazz sounds of *When Sunny Gets Blue* began. Lily Cup took Peck by the hand, turned and embraced him, and they danced from the table. She lowered a hand onto his butt and in a turn she whispered.

"So, what's up?"

"I maybe need help, cher," Peck said.

"Trouble?"

"Something I saw and what I know now."

"Is this about André?"

"Nah nah, not him, cher."

"Something we need to do now? Tonight?"

"Nah nah, not tonight," Peck said.

Lily Cup rested her head on his shoulder in thought.

"Go home. Read your books or whatever, but get your homework done so you can take tomorrow off. Meet me at the office. I'll be out of court by noon. We'll lock the door. You'll have my full attention."

Peck nodded.

Not wanting to chance disappointing Peck, Lily Cup leaned in for another whisper.

"Are you sure it'll wait?"

"It ain't goin' no place, cher."

Lily Cup air-kissed a smooch, squeezed his butt cheek, turned and headed to the empty stool next to André.

Peck pulled a chair, sat and picked up his spoon.

"That was a quick dance," Sasha said.

What Peck didn't know was that Sasha had seen Peck and André come out of the back room as she and Lily Cup were coming into Charlie's. Lily Cup had told her best friend what André was to Peck.

"Keeping secrets?" Sasha asked.

"Sasha why you wasting time sittin' here wrinkling that expensive purdy red dress when you and my frien', that beautiful ol' man sittin' here with nothin' to do should be dancing to this sweet jazz?" Peck asked.

Sasha knew when to shut up. She looked at Gabe.

"He sure turns it on when he wants to," Sasha muses.

"Peck's one of a kind," Gabe said.

"So, we dancing, or you eating beans?" she asked.

Gabe pushed the bowl away and placed his napkin over the top.

"My baby. I've been sitting here thinking you were a mirage, just a lovely beautiful dream I was having."

Sasha stood with a smile. "My girls have a way of doing that to bad boys."

"They're playing Louis and Ella, darlin'," Gabe said.

"Let's dance," Sasha said.

Gabe offered his hand.

"These earrings are killing me," Sasha said.

"Will you see Gabe gets home?" Peck asked.

Sasha looked back.

"I need to study," Peck said.

Sasha took Gabe's hand and led him to the dance floor. She pulled an earring off and nestled her head on his neck.

"I have every intention of wearing him out first"— she turned her head and looked at Peck—"but I'll get him home."

Peck spooned the last of his beans, stood and counted out eight dollars. He dropped it on the table and headed home, savoring his talk with André in his memory. He needed time, important time to think for his meetup with Lily Cup and how to tell her what he'd seen. Books always helped Peck think best, and that night especially he wanted to read what happened to Tom Joad, who'd been on the run for killing a man under the bridge.

5.

PECK FINISHED A MORNING CHICORY with Gabe, assuring him that he and Lily Cup would talk it out after her court. He walked from the house to St. Charles Avenue, crossed over the tracks and lined up behind five others as the streetcar rolled to a stop. In turn he boarded and paid. He stood and held a strap, letting others have the seats. His eyes were the cold stare of a tracker on the hunt of his life. He stepped off at Lee Circle and walked to Canal Street. He stood on the corner in thought while looking up the boulevard at the row of hotels as if they were cypress trees in a swampy bayou.

A passing car's honk woke him and he stepped off the curb and headed into the French Quarter with eyes peeled. He turned on Royal Street as though he was thinking of heading up Carrolton Avenue and backtracking to Lily Cup's offices, looking for possible witnesses. A row of pedicabs caught his eye. A dozen or so, some with female drivers, some male. He turned away, facing an antique store window. He slowly turned around. Some drivers sat in passenger compartments, some rested on the bicycle seats. Some talked, others looked at their iPhones. One pedicab was the pedicab B-25 he saw on Carrollton Avenue. What should he do next? He had to convince himself the girl pedaling B-25 last night didn't see him up in the window. Her pedicab wasn't in front. It was the seventh in line. He walked over.

"You available, cher?"

"Sure, where to?"

"Jes' a ride."

The girl gave him a curious glance. "Why this one? That first one is closer to the street."

"Twenty-five is lucky number cher, dass for true."

"You're from New Orleans, aren't you?"

"Ah *oui.*"

"So if you're from here, Dude, why do you want a ride?"

"Killin' time, cher, and I need sun and thinkin' maybe let you do the work, ha!"

Peck pulled a twenty from his pocket and held it up.

"This good for a ride, bébé?"

"It's good, but I'll tell you now, I don't talk French or any of that backward Cajun stuff, so no offense if I don't understand you."

"Where you from, cher?"

"Oklahoma."

"Been here long?"

"We talking, or do you want a ride?"

Peck reached in his pocket and pulled another twenty and held it up. The girl gave it a wary look.

"Can't we do both, cher?"

"Where do you want to go?"

"Jes' around a block or two is all."

The girl smiled, took the twenty.

"Hop in."

"Thanks, cher."

"We'll go to the river, around the park and back here, okay?"

"Perfect. What's your name?" Peck asked.

"Lauren."

"Ahh, cher, such a purdy name. I'm Peck."

"Thanks," Lauren said.

"Just around the Quarter is okay."

Lauren began pedaling, first while standing to get the pedicab up to speed and then sitting. She would look both ways crossing intersections, and if an opening happened between two cars, she would hand-signal and carefully pull behind one and follow it to the next corner.

"You own this nice pedicab, cher?" Peck asked.

"We rent it," Lauren said, panting.

"Ah. Have a partner?"

"Two of us."

"Hard work, pedaling, dass for true."

"Long as we pay on time and fix flats we can use it."

"That's a good thing. You happy with that deal?"

"It's good on football weekends when Saints play and during Mardi Gras, but it's a lot of work in slow times, like weekdays. But it's good, I guess."

"With French Quarter crazy like it is, you must work all night sometime, cher," Peck said.

"Pretty late."

"How's that work? You share with your partner or do you get a separate day?"

Lauren pedaled as a Riverfront streetcar approached.

"We take turns."

"How's that work, bébé?"

"We break up days. One day I get day, the next day I get night. We do eight hours, if we're busy."

Lauren waved at a pedicab girl coming from the opposite direction.

"Today I'm filling in for my roommate. She had a dentist appointment, and I need the money."

"You have a good thing figured out. Do you make more money on how you say, fares, cher, or on tips?"

Lauren didn't respond. She was concentrating on an upcoming turn. There was an uncomfortable look in her eyes with so much talk about money. Especially after being robbed the night before. As she looked around the corner, as if wanting to turn, she glanced at Peck, sizing him up. She kept pedaling.

"Last night, cher, after midnight, which partner was working?"

Lauren turned the wheel sharply and scratched the pedicab tire into a curb to a sudden stop. She stood and turned.

"Who are you, Dude?"

"Hanh?"

She stepped out of the cab and up on the sidewalk, out of Peck's reach and pointed across the street.

"There's a cop. Tell me what you want, or I'm going to call for him."

"I'm not a bad man, cher."

"Are you a cop?"

"Nah nah."

"So why are you asking these questions, Dude? I'm not afraid of you. I'll yell for that cop."

"I'm not bad, dass for true."

"You sound creepy, calling me cher, bébé, all that Mardi Gras make-believe put-on accent bullshit stuff. What do you want?"

Peck climbed out and stood behind the pedicab.

"I'll tell you if it was you workin' last night? If it wasn't you, I'll go away now— promise?"

"I don't know what you're talking about."

Lauren wadded and tossed one of the twenties in Peck's direction.

"Ride's over," she said. "Go away."

Peck stepped back as if he was leaving.

"Oh, bébé."

"What do you want from me?"

"Not a thing, bébé. I just want to find that girl I saw gettin' beaten up on Carrollton las night."

"Don't know what you're talking about. Goodbye."

"I want to find the man what put a gun in your face."

"Who are you?"

"I saw the black Mercedes."

"You could see us?"

"I watched it all. I want to save her life and get that man. Honest, cher."

"I hope he dies," Lauren said.

"I saw him take your money, bébé."

Peck picked up the twenty from the seat of the pedicab and held it out for her to take.

"You saw him take Tiffany?"

"Is that her name? Tiffany?"

Lauren stepped off the sidewalk.

"That's the name they make her use."

"What'cha mean, cher?"

Lauren took the twenty from his hand. She motioned for him to hop in.

"She told me that if she ever let anybody know her real name they'd kill her family first, then her. I only know her as Tiffany."

"How'd you meet her?"

"Are you for real?" Lauren asked.

"I'm for real."

Lauren got in the pedicab, pushed it back and turned the wheel. She looked back at Peck.

"A fat slob was standing with her at the corner by the Hyatt. He flagged me and gave me a fifty and told me to take her anywhere she wanted to go."

"She knew him, the fat man?"

"She told me he worked for some big movie star or producer or something."

"Did she tell you how much he paid?" Peck asked.

"She was crying."

"Did she tell you why she was crying?"

"Yeah. The movie dude was going to watch her doing a black dude and her period started and the dude wouldn't do her, so the movie prick got pissed and threw her out in ten minutes after paying for three hours."

"Gris gris," Peck mumbled.

"She wanted to run away last night. Told me her pimp would be coming to the hotel to pick her up in three hours and probably wouldn't feed her because she didn't earn the money. I bought her some food and she told me everything. Talked a mile a minute. You should have seen her asking what time it was every few minutes."

"What hotel las' night, cher?"

"I don't know. He was like ten feet away from her but on a corner. Canal Street. Could be any one of them. I pick up girls all the time coming out of hotels after doing it. Boys too."

"Why would the girls and how you say the boys who just come out of a hotel after, you know— why would they catch a pedicab like they a tourist, cher? Answer me d'at."

"I guess because they have to let people see them and hope to get another customer. Maybe their pimp makes them do that so they won't get stopped by cops walking sidewalks. I don't know, but I know if somebody whistles or yells out the girls get out and go talk to them. Sometimes their drop-off is at a pimp waiting in a car a block or two away."

"Ah *oui*."

"Dude, do I have to keep pedaling?"

"Can we talk someplace, maybe? I just want to find Tiffany. I want to save her life."

Lauren pedaled to a bicycle stand and chained the pedicab. She pointed to an outside table at Café Du Monde.

"My treat. How you like it?" Lauren asked.

"Two sugars, bébé. Thanks."

Lauren came out with coffees.

"So, you saw everything last night?"

"I was working in a building. The window was open, and I heard a scream, and then I saw him hit her."

"He smacked her. Severe Epistaxis, all blood."

"Hanh?"

"Nosebleed, I learned that in nursing school."

"After you left, he beat her hard," Peck said.

"That bastard. I hope he dies."

"Ah *oui*."

"Could you really see me?"

"Not your face good, but I saw his gun and I saw him take your money."

"I thought I was dead for sure."

"I was afraid to do anything, cher, thinkin' he might shoot you and Tiffany if he saw me. I was afraid, I'll say."

"I shook all night, wondering if I could ever work in a trauma center," Lauren said. "I still worry about her."

"They went to Storyville. I followed them."

"She told me that's where they lived."

"You mean the man and Tiffany?"

"I don't know about the bastard, but Tiffany and other girls. Boys too. She told me they had to you know, do whoever they told them to."

"Aye-yi-yi."

"Tiffany has to sex eight, ten guys a day or she gets no food."

"They're slaves," Peck said.

"They drug the boys with a needle every night. One is seven years old and a lady walks him into hotels like she's his school teacher and waits in the hall while somebody does whatever to him."

"Why don't they run away, cher?"

"For the girls they threaten to tell all their friends and family what they do and show pictures, or they threaten to kill their families. Tiffany told me they get the boys so hooked on something they will need another needle every ten hours and they never run away."

"Where he from, I wonder?" Peck asked. "The movie man."

"Tiffany said he has a house in the Garden District, but he does sex with kids in suites."

"Suites?"

"Fancy hotel suites, not at his house. You ever heard of Hamptons?"

"Is that a place?"

"Yes."

"Nah-nah. How you spell it, cher?"

"H-A-M-T-O-N-S, I guess. Tiffany told me that's where he's from."

Lauren lifted her iPhone and made a search.

"It's H-A-M-P-T-O-N-S. Hamptons. Says here it's on Long Island. That's in New York."

"He lives where?"

"Both, I guess. Hamptons and New Orleans."

"Rich man."

"She told me she was running away. She told me what she did and that there was never money for her. Not even tip money. They pay on an iPhone and keep it secret from the cops."

"That's so they don't catch him paying a girl," Peck said.

"She begged me to help her run and wanted to work with me. I figured she had a couple of hours to get away, so I was taking her to my place when they caught us."

"What if you see Tiffany again?"

"I'd be too scared to ride her."

"I can see that, for true."

"If I even keep doing this after last night, I'm going to feel sorry, sure, but I'll be afraid to talk to any of them."

"You want to help Peck find Tiffany?"

"Not if I'll get caught like last night."

"You won't get caught, bébé."

"Like who will know I'm helping you?"

"Nobody."

"Are you sure? These people kill people."

"Just you and me, cher, nobody else."

"I'll help."

"How old is Tiffany, did she tell you?"

"Thirteen."

Peck held his fist to his mouth.

"She told me she ran away from a foster home when she was nine. A woman found her homeless and sat down on the sidewalk next to her and woke her up. Acting all friendly like she gave her a Happy Meal sack and talked to her like a mother. She promised to buy her stuff, took her home and bought her a coat, some clothes and new shoes."

"Here? New Or-lee-anh, cher?"

"Atlanta. The lady brought her and two other girls here for a vacation. Told them she was taking them to New Orleans to buy them all pretty bracelets. That's what she told them. Tiffany remembered them going up a bunch of stairs someplace and watching a man count out fifteen one-hundred-dollar bills each for two of the girls. Another man yanked one of the girls to a sofa and raped her while the man was counting out thirty one-hundred-dollar bills for Tiffany, because she was virgin. She had to pull up her dress while he pulled her panties down and inspected her. Then he made her sit on the floor and watch him rape the second girl.

Tiffany told me he said he owned her until he paid him back the money he paid for her, plus interest since she was ten."

"We got to save her, cher."

"Guess who took her cherry."

"Hanh?"

"Her cherry. Guess who took it."

"Hamptons, cher?"

"Yeah—movie man. They dressed her up in an expensive wedding gown, painted her face and everything when she was nine. She had to let him do her. Now him and whoever he says she has to do so he can watch when he's in New Orleans."

"Did she tell you the hotel?"

"It was at his house when she was virgin. They blindfolded her when they took her there, and when they took her away. She remembered a lot of turns and remembered hearing a streetcar."

"Je veux le nourrir en direct aux gators." ("I want to feed him live to gators.")

"Look, I only came here to get away from an old boyfriend I broke up with and save some money for my last year in nursing school. I just want to save enough and get out of here. If they find out she told me they'll kill her and me."

"He take your money."

"It was my rent money too."

"What bag did you have last night, cher?"

Lauren held her bag up. "This one."

"It'll have his fingerprints on it, cher."

Lauren dropped the bag on the table.

"Eww," she said.

"Maybe my frien' find who this man is with prints."

"Can anyone find out he got them from my bag? Labs can trace things, you know?"

"No. I promise, cher."

Lauren opened the bag, stuffed her pockets. She handed the bag to Peck, using two fingers.

"Here."

Peck delicately wrapped it in paper napkins.

"We need a signal," Peck said.

"A signal?"

"For when we want to talk," Peck said.

"Like what kind of signal?"

"Let me think on it."

"We can text," Lauren said.

"Nah nah, they can trace that. I'll find you this week and come up with something."

"Okay."

"When you work days, cher?"

"Tomorrow and Friday this week. Monday I stay home and study my nursing manuals."

"I'll find you."

Peck finished his coffee.

"If I walk up and hand you a twenty dollar bill, cher, take it. Make it look real."

"You have a girlfriend?" Lauren asked.

Peck leaned down.

"The best thing we do to stay safe is to not know about each other. We help Tiffany first—we can't weaken our advantage or anything."

"I was only asking."

"Best we be secret until it's over."

"You're right. Find her and get her out of that place."

"You dance, cher?"

"I like Zydeco."

"Oh mon cher, fais do-do." ("Oh my dear, a dance party.")

"You Zydeco?"

"I have a girlfriend, love of my life, dass for true—but you're special, cher. You have pretty hair like my frien' Elizabeth in Baton Rouge."

"I do?"

"We get Tiffany safe, and you and me we'll go dance, okay? You can teach me Zydeco, bébé. Jimmy Broussard say I'd like it, dass for true."

Lauren smiled.

Peck held up the bag. "I'll get this back, bébé."

"I'm sorry for what I said about your accent. You know … how you talk."

"S'okay, cher. I grew up in a swamp. It's all I got."

He turned and started to walk away.

"But I read the dictionary ever' day, dass for true."

"You need a ride?" Lauren asked.

"Nah-nah, but thanks, cher. Peck needs to look around some more."

"Bye," Lauren said. "Thanks for helping Tiffany."

6.

AS PECK GOT OFF THE ELEVATOR at the law offices, Lily Cup was in the break room, pouring coffee into a thermos.

"How was court today, cher?" Peck asked.

She nodded for Peck to follow her back to her office. He stepped in, and she pulled the door closed behind her. She handed the thermos to Peck and took her coat off.

"You pour, Peck. Cups and paninis are on the desk. I hope you like Cajun chicken."

"I like chicken, cher."

Lily Cup stepped out of her heels, turned and plopped back into what was once her father's oversized leather wingback desk chair. Her skirt rode up her thighs as she crossed her legs like a tomboy by a campfire.

"How was court?" Peck asked again.

"Listen to this one, Peck. It's about midnight and a man was driving on Magazine Street and someone jumped in the back seat, shot him and then jumped out. So, the man who got shot and had a bullet in his back drove into a convenience store parking lot and fell out of his car to the ground. So, they called the cops and a cop came, leaned on one knee and the man said, 'Avril did it, it was Avril that shot me.'"

"…and?" Peck asked.

"And the cop never asked who Avril was."

"That happen in court?"

"Wait, there's more."

"Okay."

"Another cop does a line-up in the man's hospital room. This time it was a lady cop, and she took four pictures into the man's room for identification. She held them up and pointed to one and said, 'We think this is the guy who shot you.'"

"She didn't let the man pick the shooter, cher?"

"The cop said she had to do it that way because the man in the hospital bed couldn't point because he couldn't move his arms."

"Aye-yi-yi!" Peck said.

"So, the judge asked to watch the tape, watched it and saw the man moving his arms under his blanket."

Peck set a half-eaten panini on the desk and took a long look at Lily Cup. It was a kind of look that said he was ready to talk, and according to Gabe she was key to his helping the girl he watched Sunday night.

"Smoke you a cigar, cher," Peck said.

He stood and pulled the window up a foot.

Lily Cup raised her brow at his facial expression. Was he being cordial or was he beginning a tracking mode? In either case she knew Peck, and she would have known he had just signaled he was ready to be serious. She lifted a bare thigh for balance, reached for the cigar box on her desk and for her platinum clipper. She took a cigar and sat back. With her thumb and index finger she rolled the phallic cigar in and out of her wet lips on a curved moist tongue. Her thumb flicked twice and her lighter sparked flame. She lifted her thigh, again for balance, and returned the lighter to the desk before bouncing back in the wingback.

"Talk to me, Peck."

"Let me think where to start, cher."

"Take your time. Nothing on my calendar."

"I was cleaning Sunday night. I come down like I always do to open your window to air out your office. I hear this yelling down on the street and I saw a man with a girl he was saying was his whore. He was beating her for leaving Storyville. He slugged her, cher. Then he pushed his gun in the pedicab girl's face and he took her money and tol' her go away or he'd shoot her."

"You saw this from my window?" Lily Cup asked.

"*Oui.*"

"What time was it?"

"Like 1:43. Didn't André—?" Peck started.

"Now, now, Peck."

"Hanh?"

"You know I can't talk about what André and I talk about. Client privilege."

"I followed the car."

"Where to?"

"Storyville."

"Jesus, Peck, Storyville is deadly at that hour."

"I got a license plate. I knew where that pimp and girl walked into."

Lily Cup lifted her thigh, reached and took the pad and pen from her desk and sat back with hands free and the cigar in her mouth.

"Give it," Lily Cup said.

"The address?"

"The plate number."

"The pedicab number was 25-B," Peck said.

"No, the car plate," Lily Cup said.

Peck told her the number.

"Hold on," Lily Cup said.

Lily Cup made a call to a Lieutenant Detective Larry Gaines, the tall black detective who helped Gabe get out of murder charges the year before. Detective Gaines took the time to find the knife Gabe was threatened with after others had given up. She repeated the plate number over the phone, waited a few minutes, and then scratched some notes on her pad, listening to someone on the other end.

"Thanks, Larry." She ended the call.

"Who was that?" Peck asked.

"A detective I know."

"Thanks, cher."

"What kind of car was it, Peck?"

"A black Mercedes."

"Ready for this?"

"*Oui.*"

"The plates were stolen from a Honda Civic."

"Hanh?"

"They found them on a Mercedes this morning."

"Where, cher?"

"Where did you follow it to?"

"Storyville first but then I followed it to Canal Street. It went in a parking garage at a hotel on Canal Street."

"Did you go to Metairie?"

"Nah-nah, not Metairie, cher."

"At three a.m. this morning they found the Mercedes in front of a bookstore in Metairie."

"Hanh?"

"It was abandoned."

"Empty?"

"It was sitting on its rims on the ground."

"I wonder why, cher?"

"Someone probably stole the tires."

"Nah-nah, why Metairie?"

"Cops are trying to figure that out," Lily Cup said. "There's no trace of the Honda Civic or its owner."

"Maybe somebody stole the Mercedes from the hotel and didn't want to get caught," Peck said.

"They won't tell me who owned the Mercedes. It's evidence," Lily Cup said.

"Why would an expensive car be abandoned, cher?"

"There's more, Peck."

"Like what?"

"They found blood on the front seat."

"Aye-yi-yi," Peck said. "Maybe that's why."

"Did anyone see you watching them, Peck?"

"Lights were off here," Peck said.

"Where did you follow them?"

"All over until Canal Street. A hotel."

"It's getting spooky," Lily Cup said.

"Cher, think they saw me following? Storyville— then to Canal Street?"

"My guess is with them staying at an expensive hotel, they've got money. Rich people can pay for protection, Peck. They'll pay for eyes and ears."

"What's that mean?"

"If you followed them, they'll have your plate and maybe got a good look at you."

"I was careful."

"You knew they had a gun, Peck, what the fuck were you thinking?"

"The girl is a kid, cher, thirteen."

"How would you know she's thirteen?"

"I jes' know, cher."

"What are you not telling me?"

"I jes' know is all."

"What do you want from me, Peck? I'm not a cop."

"The girl needs help."

"What are you reading?"

"Hanh?"

"For Tulane, what are you reading?"

"You mean what book?"

"Yes."

"I just finished *Grapes of Wrath*, why?"

"Because I know you, Peck."

"What'cha mean, cher?"

"I knew something had to possess you to do something stupid, like follow a car you knew had guns in it. What was it in *Grapes of Wrath* that made you want to follow murderers to Canal Street at 1:45 in the morning?"

"Tom Joad."

"Tom Joad? Wasn't he the one who had that, 'I'll be there' quote about America's downtrodden?"

"I won't lie," Peck said.

"Killed a man, memory serving me," Lily Cup said. "Didn't Tom Joad kill somebody?"

"Dass for true, cher. Conked him under the bridge."

"What's on your mind, Peck?"

"I know where the man lives, I think, cher."

"I'm a lawyer, Peck. There's no way in hell I can play any part in—" Lily Cup started.

"I was a slave, cher."

Lily Cup paused—two fingers pulled the cigar from her lips.

"What's your point?"

"The girl needs help. She's a slave."

"And?" Lily Cup asked.

"That pimp got to be stopped, cher."

"There's blood on the front seat of an abandoned car, Peck—looks like somebody's been stopped," Lily Cup said.

"She was in the back seat."

"How many were in the car, Peck?"

"Windows were dark. I couldn't see."

Lily Cup's face became ashen. She nervously rolled the wet cigar in pouted lips. She stared through Peck's eyes as if she remembered how helpless criminal courts were in curbing human trafficking, how much trouble she could get into by helping Peck avenge a man he watched beat a girl. His eyes frightened her. They were telling eyes, telling her he wouldn't stop his hunt.

"I need a rye," Lily Cup mumbled.

"Will you help me, cher?"

"I need a tall rye," Lily Cup said, leaning forward to reach a lower left desk drawer where she kept bottles. "Let me ask you something, Peck."

"Okay, ax."

"That pimp-dude walked in here right now, what would you do?"

"I'd tie him with fishing line."

"So, you wouldn't kill him?"

"Not here."

"I was afraid you'd say that."

"Don't you want him dead too, cher?"

"I want to warn people, Peck. I want to find out how to educate them. We're not talking murder here."

"I'd heat a knife blade red hot with your cigar lighter cher. I'd brand 'GORILLA' on his forehead."

"Gorilla?"

"It's money, cher. It's money what they kidnap girls and boys for and it's a *blade* where people go pay money for sexin' girls and boys. Gabe told me about it all. That red dollar tattoo pimp is a *gorilla*, dass for true, because he beats her but that fat man at the fancy hotel whose movie man boss pays for sex is a trafficker too."

"Fat man!? Movie man!? Goddammit Peck, what are you hiding from me?"

"The movie man don't think he's a trafficker because he pays for sex. He don't think he steals kids—but if he puts up money for sex he's payin' for people to steal them. If a kid see *gorilla* branded on a forehead, they'd run for sure."

Lily Cup stood, snuffed her cigar in the ashtray and adjusted her skirt on her thighs. "Finish your sandwich. I'll be right back," she said.

She stepped from the office and disappeared. She returned to find Peck looking down on Carrolton Avenue.

"You're scaring the hell out of me, Peck."

"You think they saw me, cher?"

"No telling, but I wouldn't bet they didn't."

"Where'd you go?" Peck asked.

"I had to pee…"

"Ahh," Peck said.

"And think."

Peck bit into his panini.

"I don't know what you're keeping from me, but I can't worry about that right now," Lily Cup said. "I have an idea."

"What?"

"Do you still run?"

"Ah *oui*."

"Where's your gear?"

"In my pickup, why?"

"Move the thermos and your sandwich off the desk. I want to show you something."

Lily Cup took a city map, unfolded it broadside and flattened it on the desk.

"Take a look," Lily Cup said.

Peck stepped around the desk and looked at the map of New Orleans. With a pen as her pointer, Lily Cup pointed at the address of her law offices.

"Here's where we are now."

She moved the pointer slowly.

"Here's the French Quarter …"

"Ah *oui*."

"Here's Bourbon Street …"

"Ah *oui*."

"These are the streets to Storyville. See here? Storyville is—what does it say on the mileage scale? Let's say it's two, maybe two and a half miles. Can you run that far and back, Peck?"

"Ah *oui*."

Lily Cup folded the map, placed it on the shelf and plopped in her chair. She yanked her skirt up her thighs, rested one foot on the desk, bent her other leg at the knee and rested the other foot on her chair seat. Peck sat and waited, taking in the art of her bare inner thighs.

"You remember everywhere you went that night?" Lily Cup asked.

"Ah *oui*."

"I mean everywhere you followed them?"

"Ah *oui*."

"Here's the deal, Peck."

"Okay."

"My better judgment is telling me to tell you you're on your own, that's what my gut's telling me."

"Okay, cher. If that's how you think."

"I need your promise that you're going to listen."

"I'll listen good, cher."

"I need your word you'll remember what I'm about to tell you."

"You have Peck's word, cher."

"I want to help, but there's got to be rules—you have to believe I could get in serious trouble for conspiracy."

"Ah *oui*," Peck said. "I know *conspire*, cher."

"There can't be any money from me or from this law office that can tie us in—"

"I understand," Peck said.

"Not a penny."

"Ah *oui*."

"And after today no talk about it here— in this office. I can't afford getting entangled in anything that could lose my license, get me disbarred or worse."

Peck didn't speak.

"You're a native-born tracker, Peck. We're going to use that to our advantage."

Peck didn't respond.

"You know swamps. You've had to learn how to observe just to survive. Gabe told me you're the best he'd ever seen at observation in all his years in the military. You don't miss a thing."

Peck didn't respond.

"I have a hunch. I want to play it out."

Peck waited.

"I want you to retrace the route you drove following that car."

"Okay."

"But this time I want you to run it. Jog it."

"I can do that, cher."

Wherever you went that night, through the French Quarter, Bourbon Street, Storyville."

"Okay."

"And keep your eyes open."

"Ah *oui*."

"Go change into your running gear. Pretend you're in a pirogue, tracking for alligators. It'll be the same, only this time you're running the streets of N'Orleans, watching for sex trafficking signs."

"How you mean, signs, cher?"

"The danger signs. Could be college girls like Millie drinking too much—somebody pouring them free drinks or following them on a sidewalk. Sex for sale is trafficking— so it could be a massage parlor. It could be a mother letting her kid get too far away from her side in a store or park. They sell babies too. Could be a streetwalker. Could be a titty bar."

"What do I do if I see something?"

"Just remember what and where it was."

"Ah *oui*."

"Make a count of the 'blades' you see …"

"I can did that."

"And meet me at the house after."

"Your house?"

"My house."

"I got to study tonight, cher."

"Not tonight, Peck. You did your studying last night. We had a deal."

"Okay."

"I'll cook."

Lily Cup stood, adjusted her skirt down, reached and lifted a heavy bronze cane from a hook behind her desk.

"This was Daddy's cane."

"It's beautiful, cher."

"Take it."

"Why?"

"You may need it. The handle unscrews. It has an umbrella inside."

"Ah *oui*. Thanks, cher."

"This is N'Orleans, Peck. Never know when a heavy umbrella might come in handy."

Lily Cup handed Peck the cane.

"Go change, leave your clothes and keys with me."

"Okay."

"Finish the run at my house."

Lily Cup gripped Peck's waistband and pulled him close.

"You remember André's story about what happened to gator man, Peck?" Lily Cup whispered.

"Ah *oui*."

"From this moment on, my house is the only safe place to talk about this without being heard, understand?"

"Ah *oui*, cher. I understand."

"We're going to be bosom buddies until it's over. Until we free the girl."

"Ah *oui*."

"I'll have your pickup in my driveway."

"Okay, good."

"Let me see your key fob."

Peck handed her his keys.

"Do any of these buttons start it?"

"Ah *oui,* cher. Push this button two times and this 'un one time and it starts. The saleslady told me Detroit is cold, and in the winter they start trucks and cars to warm up."

"Remember what I'm about to tell you, Peck."

"What?"

"Make sure there's no one standing near your pickup, but always start it before you get to it."

"Why, cher?"

"Sex trafficking is a billion-dollar business."

"Ah *oui.*"

"Billions."

"Ah *oui.*"

"If those people saw your plate following them."

"They have guns, cher."

"Peck there's a lot of money behind them. They'll leave no evidence or clues. Guns leave clues."

"Ah *oui,*" Peck said.

"Boom," Lily Cup said.

"For true, cher?"

"These bastards wouldn't think twice about wiring a pickup with a car bomb. That thirteen-year-old girl makes them a thousand bucks a day, seven days a week. They give her a bed, a dress and maybe five bucks in food. They wouldn't think twice about taking out the driver of a pickup who had the balls to follow them."

"Thanks for bein' smart for Peck."

"I have calls to make. Homework of my own," Lily Cup said.

Peck stepped to the door.

"Work up an appetite. Remember we're eating at the house tonight," Lily Cup said.

Peck went outside, stood away from his pickup and started it. He changed in the men's room and went into Lily Cup's office in running attire and handed her the key fob and running bag with his clothes.

"Here, cher. I see you later."
Lily Cup checked his abs and thighs and smiled.
"You have an ID, money?"
"I got my license," Peck said. He patted a pocket.
Lily Cup opened her purse, took four twenties from it and stepped over to Peck.
"This is a loan."
She reached and tugged his waistband and dropped the folded twenties in and let it go with a snap.
"Never go anywhere without cash," Lily Cup said.
"Thanks, cher. I have money in this bag. Pay yourself back."
"You're maybe staying tonight?"
"Maybe, cher."
"Should I tell Gabe?"
"He knows, cher. He knows I might not be home."
Lily Cup smiled.
"Peck?"
"Ah *oui*?"
"Be careful."

7.

PECK'S JOG ENDED in front of Lily Cup's house. He walked up the driveway, stepped around his pickup and up to the side kitchen door. Lily Cup let a sweaty, panting, bare-chested Peck in.

"Hot damn," Lily Cup said with a smile.

As he came through the door she teasingly slid a palm on his glistening chest and copped a feel.

"Have a good run?"

"Ah *oui.*"

"Learn anything?"

"A lot, cher."

"You want to shower?"

"Ah *oui.*"

"Go up and shower. We'll eat, then we'll talk."

"Okay."

"I put your clothes in the second bedroom."

"Thanks, cher."

"Need me to wash your back?"

Peck grinned and started to leave the kitchen.

"Hold on a sec. I need a baking dish."

Lily Cup opened two upper cabinets.

"Daddy was our cook and he was tall. Top shelf, Peck. Can you reach that baking dish."

As Peck reached Lily Cup checked out his thighs and calves.

"I hope Millie appreciates what she's got," Lily Cup whispered.

Peck handed her the baking dish with a grin.

"Are you *objectifying* me, cher?"

Lily Cup howled.

"Where the fuck did you learn that?"

"Gabe I think."

"Speaking of Gabe—know what tonight's about?"

"Helping a girl, cher?"

"That too, but tonight, is about calming you down."

"Hanh?"

"Gabe and I talked and we agreed. We've got to slow your pace. It's going to get you in trouble if you don't slow down. I'm talking serious Angola trouble, getting the needle trouble."

"What you cooking, cher?"

"When I went by your house to talk with Gabe, he gave me some redfish you caught. I'm going to poach them. Buttery lemon and cream sauce."

"My favorite," Peck said.

"You can shuck the oysters when you come down."

"Gabe knows I'm here?"

"Yep."

"He say anything?"

"Yep."

"What he say, cher?"

"Want the truth?"

"Ah *oui*."

"He said 'the boy's a born tracker.' He said if you've been running and tracking all day, I'm just to let you open up on your own without prodding. I'm to wait for whatever you come up with on your own from your run."

"Gabe a smart man, dass for true."

"Good idea then?"

"Ah *oui*."

"Go shower. I'll bring you a beer."

Lily Cup prepped the baking dish and sat it on the counter. She'd put it in the preheated oven when Peck came down. It'd be a few minutes to bake. She'd calm Peck's mind with opening salvos of raw oysters with horseradish cocktail sauce and with sliced garden tomatoes with balsamic glaze. Lily Cup heard the shower turn off, poured a beer in a glass and went up to the second floor and saw a naked Peck toweling off in the guest bedroom. She savored the moment.

"Brought you a beer."

Holding a towel to his chest Peck turned toward her.

"Jesus, you're gorgeous," Lily Cup said.

With a blank look he let her watch, almost as if he was in the wilds and nudity was not an issue. Lily Cup handed him the beer and looked him in the eye.

"Stay tonight? I'll be good, I promise."

Peck watched her eyes.

"Stay here?" Lily Cup asked.

Peck held out the towel for her to take.

"Okay."

Lily Cup traded the beer for the towel, glanced at Peck's William, and backed out of the room.

"See you downstairs," Lily Cup said.

Standing in the kitchen they took turns. Peck would shuck an oyster and feed it to Lily Cup, and she'd stab a sliced wedge of tomato, dipped it in glaze, and feed it to him. The two had a close bond from the first night they met way more than a year ago.

Peck was an illiterate Cajun French lawn-mowing hunk who first walked into Charlie's with Gabe the night she was drinking rye before a murder trial the next day. She was so smitten with him she sobered up on Charlie's black coffee long enough to seduce Peck in the ladies room while Gabe danced for four hours with Sasha. That all happened the first night they met. The four of them have had an unshakable bond ever since.

Lily Cup baked and served the dinner and they savored the butter and lemon on the flakey fish. New Orleans dining is an experience, not to be interrupted by distractions. They sat and ate in silence.

Dinner finished, plates still on the table, Lily Cup brought out an unopened bottle of rye and a half-bottle of Courvoisier brandy. She stacked the plates, took them to the kitchen and brought out two crystal glasses, one an etched tumbler and one a smooth, paper-thin crystal triple shot glass. She poured a glass of a brandy for him and a glass of rye for herself and sat at the table by the corner.

"Cheers," Lily Cup said, holding up her glass.

They clicked glasses and each took a hearty gulp.

"Who goes first?" Lily Cup asked.

Peck took another swig.

"You go first, cher. Then I'll go."

"I learned a lot today," Lily Cup said. "I talked to a lot of people. The sheriff, police chief, even a state trooper in Lafayette working on trafficking. The N'Orleans mayor suggested I talk with the District Attorney. Want to hear?"

"Ah *oui*."

They both took a sip.

"It's legal to record conversations if both parties approve—he approved.

Peck sipped another slug of his brandy and set the glass down.

Lily Cup went to her purse and retrieved a pencil thin recorder.

"This thing will record eight hours."

She sat, rested her elbow and held it up after pressing a button. The recorder played.

"Lily Cup Tarleton here, how are you?"

"I spoke with the mayor this morning."

"Good people, a good mayor."

"The mayor suggested I ask you for ideas."

"How can I help, Counselor?"

"I'm considering being on the mayor's taskforce on human trafficking. Any advice?"

"It's a mess. What advice you have in mind?"

"I don't know where to start."

"What's the taskforce's objective?"

"Public awareness?"

"That's what the police chief suggested."

"That's like saying illicit sex can be stopped by shedding light on it. Prostitution is the oldest trade. Sex with

children is the same. The kids don't consent, but you will not stop the market for it. Pedophilia is not going to be eradicated. Just like rape isn't."

Lily Cup took a slug of rye.

"Drug dealers have moved to trafficking women for sex as it's more profitable than drugs. Inventory keeping is cheaper till she dies if she can have sex ten times a day. They just have to make it a harsher punishment."

Lily Cup stopped the recorder. Peck looked as if he was tracking in his brain. Lily Cup sipped her rye, waited for him to open up and make his report. He gulped his brandy, lifted the bottle and filled his tumbler again. He lifted it to make a toast. Lily Cup poured more rye and raised her glass and they clicked.

"You sayin' we drinkin' to people by teachin' them about bad people, cher?"

Lily Cup smiled at a less impulsive, more sensible Peck. She tipped her glass and swallowed her rye.

"Cher?" Peck asked with a slur.

"What?"

"Les' go to bed."

"It's only ten-thirty. Aren't you going to tell me about your day?" Lily Cup hiccupped. "About your run?"

"Your bed, cher?"

Lily Cup stood up. With a bit of a weave, she bent over and tugged her tights down to the floor and stepped out of them with a grin. She pulled the T-shirt off over her head and dropped it. She stood braless in black panties.

"You have nice *tetines*, cher."

Lily Cup blushed, pressing palms on her breasts.

"Follow me," she said.

Peck stood and unzipped his jeans. He dropped them to the floor and stepped out of them commando and kicked them under the table while he pulled off his T-shirt. He approached Lily Cup naked and held a bottle out for her to take from him.

"Here," Peck said.

She took it, reached to the table and picked up the rye bottle in her other hand.

Peck cradled her like Rhett lifted Scarlett in *Gone with the Wind*, and carried her up the stairs. On the second floor landing she pointed the rye bottle like a compass needle at her bedroom door. By the time they rested on her bed in the dark they were kissing passionately. Lily Cup moaned lust-filled murmurs as they kissed. She felt his back, his shoulders with her palms, clutched his muscular butt cheeks while she devoured his tongue.

Lily Cup had waited for this for a long time, but she knew she was Peck's friend first and it had to be his first move. She liked Millie immensely, and she knew deep down she wouldn't risk either friendship. Peck's William throbbed like a door knocker on the back of her thigh. Lily Cup reached behind and felt it with slow, gentle fingertip grips pulling it, stroking its shaft, its head. She felt herself. She was wet.

"Wait, Peck."

Peck licked her neck.

"Peck, hold on."

He paused in the dark. Lily Cup let go of William, reached out and turned the bedside lamp on. Peck squinted in its light.

"We can't fuck, Peck."

"Hanh?"

"Well, we could, but it wouldn't be right."

Peck reached for the bottle of rye, took the cork out with his teeth and handed the bottle to Lily Cup. She tipped it back proudly. Peck tilted it from the bottom of the bottle with his thumb for her next swig.

"I know, cher."

She swallowed and ran her middle finger across her lips like it was a napkin while smirking coyly.

"Can we maybe just fool around?"

Peck didn't respond.
"You be okay with a little fooling around, Peck?"
Peck lifted her from his chest and suckled her nipple.
"I'm guessing that's a yes," Lily Cup whimpered.

8.

EXCEPT FOR A MOCKINGBIRD'S SHARP TRILLS outside the window, waking Lily Cup, she was contented, lying on her side, her butt cheeks nestled into the warm curves of Peck's stomach. Lily Cup opened her eyes. The sun streaked to the floor through tilted blinds. Her phone said 7:00 a.m., and her calendar was blank. She reached behind and clutched his butt cheek. She smiled, reminiscing about the almost perfect evening, a night to remember. She listened to him moan a yawn.

"Are you okay?" Lily Cup asked.

"What'd we drink las' night, cher?"

"All of it, I think."

His warm hand reached around in front of her, softly feeling her breasts, her nipples, her bare stomach and pubic hair.

"What'd we do las' night, cher?"

"What didn't we do?" Lily Cup mused. "But I was a good girl and you were a good boy—we didn't do the big—you know."

Peck rolled onto his back. "You hungry, cher?"

"Are you?"

Lily Cup turned and leaned on an elbow enough to look in his face. She reached under the sheet and cupped his balls in her hand with a lustful squeeze while kissing him on the nose.

"I snacked," she whispered with smiling eyes.

Peck grinned.

"I'll make breakfast," Lily Cup said. "Quick shower and I'll cook something. You rest. We'll plan the day over breakfast and then we'll go from there."

"Okay."

"You still haven't told me anything about your run."

"I know. I will."

"Peck?"

"Ah *oui*?"

"What's the first thing on your mind today?"

Peck looked at a morning William tenting under the top sheet and smiled.

"Not that, you bad boy. What's the first thing on your mind about what we're here for?"

"You first, cher. What's on your mind first thing?"

"Well, okay. It's like what Gabe said, I'm thinking we slowed you down a little. That's a good thing."

Peck smiled.

"Your turn," Lily Cup said. "What's first for you?"

"Fingerprints, cher."

"What!?"

Lily Cup jumped out of bed and stood naked.

"Fingerprints …?"

She grabbed a pillow.

"No! Wait! Don't tell me now," Lily Cup said. "I don't want to know yet. Hold it for breakfast. I've got to be awake for this."

Peck smiled. Lily Cup hugged the pillow with a new morning modesty and backed out of the bedroom with a sheepish grin.

9.

LILY CUP CAME DOWN THE STAIRS in red panties and a Harvard Law T-shirt with shower-damp hair wrapped with a towel. She glanced at her black tights and T-shirt on the floor by the dining room table. She picked them up and put them on a chair seat for a laundry bag later. Peck's clothes weren't on the floor. She poured coffee when she heard Peck rustling up on the second floor and held a cup out for him as she watched him come down the stairs, fully dressed.

"Good morning running man."

"How you are, cher?"

"Gabe told me to let you talk on your own time, Peck. At your own speed."

"I remember you sayin' that."

"Eat some eggs and talk when you want."

"Okay."

"I made soft scrambled, chives, some garlic, okay?"

Peck nodded as he sipped coffee.

"Cher, I saw some things yesterday."

"I knew you would. That's what it was all about."

"I saw things I don't remember seein' before. It was almost like I had new eyes."

"That's because you're more aware of what's going down out there now. It's kind of like when you buy a new car you start to see a lot of the same cars on the road."

"Ah *oui*."

"It's because you're keen on it."

"I see. Dass for true."

"I knew you'd see what's in people's faces every day, like massage parlors, titty bars, the streetwalkers. That's life in the French Quarter. The life in the core of the Big Easy we've grown immune to."

"Ah *oui*."

"Did you get to Storyville?"

"*Oui*, but I saw a lot more than all that, cher."

"More? Like what?"

"Four things, mostly."

"You only saw four things? I don't get it."

"Nah nah, cher. What I mean is maybe I see a bigger how-you-say different look at things. I saw a big picture."

"Like what?"

"I saw all those things you say, but yesterday I saw how it happens too."

"Is this a fisher thing, Peck?"

"If you know where crawfish snake hide and how he attack, you can know his blind spot."

"You're losing me, Peck."

"More important, cher, you know the blind spot of the crawfish he eats."

"Crawfish have a blind spot? Give me a break."

"The crawfish snake bites the crawfish tail first, then he eat from the tail up, dass for true. That way the crawfish can't defend itself or hurt the snake with its claws."

Lily Cup looked speechless.

"I saw rich people, I saw poor people. I saw beggar poor, cher."

"We have a lot of poverty."

"But the—how-you-say—tourists, I could tell street-smart and street-stupid."

"You said four things, Peck."

"Rich and poor is two. Street-smart and street-stupid is two."

"Oh."

"That's four, cher."

"Your mind is fucking amazing."

"That's what I saw."

"Pretty simple."

"Bein' rich ain't a bad thing cher, but it's the bad rich people looking for poor people that's bad. It's street-smart people looking for street-stupid people."

"In the bad world out there, Peck, what do those four things mean to you?"

"Hunter and prey, cher."

"Damn."

"We're animals, cher."

"It's a feral world," Lily Cup said.

"Man is the only animal who kill or capture for sport or money, cher. I learned that at Tulane."

"That's why sex slavery is alive and well," Lily Cup said. "And because parents don't teach what my momma taught me … never talk to strangers. What my daddy used to teach me, never trust anybody, ever. The minute you let your guard down, they'll find some way to get in your pants. The minute they you do, most men are looking over the fence at their next conquest. Teachers lecture on not being a bully and not body shaming, but they don't teach you that a stranger would grab you in a heartbeat, from a park, from a grocery store, from a bar, and you'd be locked in a cellar for the rest of your life fucking strangers, ten a day."

"It's easy pickings out there, cher. Lures is money like André used to get gator man dead. Pimps lure poor kids and street-stupid school and college girls into traps."

"Once trapped, they never get out," Lily Cup said. "All the law does is post 800 numbers to call if you're being slaved. What good is an 800 number to a nine-year-old scared to death locked in a cellar somewhere with no phone and no clue where she is?"

"Long as somebody payin' for sex, none, cher."

"The DA was right," Lily Cup said.

"Girl gettin' beaten on Carrolton is Tiffany," Peck said.

"What?!" Lily Cup asked.

"They made her use that name. If she told her real name they'd kill her."

"How do you know this?"

Peck didn't respond.

"You're beginning to piss me off, keeping secrets."

"A woman in Atlanta saw her sleepin' on a sidewalk. She was nine and the lady gave her food. She tol' the little girl she wanted to take care of her sure, to buy things, coat and clothes. She dressed her purdy, like she was adopting her. Then she drove the girl to New Or-lee-anh and sold her to that red dollar sign tattooed pimp man I saw. She was a virgin. She was nine, cher. That woman sold the girl for three thousand dollars cash. The little girl watched the lady smile while red dollar sign counted out three thousand dollars. Ever since, that little girl has to sex ten men ever' day and earn a thousand or not eat."

Lily Cup let a tear run down her cheek. Peck stared into his coffee. His fork dropped from limp fingers onto his plate.

"I bet that bad lady in Atlanta steals young girls and boys like that all the time and sells them," Peck said.

"You're holding something in."

"I've got to, cher, or leave and not bother you."

"Your rules, Peck. I'm okay with that."

"I saw her yesterday, cher."

"You saw who? The Atlanta lady?"

"Nah, nah."

"The girl?"

"Ah *oui*."

"The same girl?"

"Ah *oui*."

"How do you know it was her?"

"The nose ring, the shorts, and her hair."

"Where'd you see her?"

"Never mind, cher. I saw her get in a car and the car pulled in an alley and parked."

"She was in the car in an alley?"

"Ah *oui*."

"Was she doing him?"

"Ah *oui*. They was doin' something."

"Did anybody see you?"

"Cher, can you get fingerprints looked at?"

"I hate when you do that, Peck."

"What?"

"Cut me off like that."

"Can you get fingerprints looked at, cher?"

"I wondered when you were going to talk about the fingerprints," Lily Cup said.

Lily Cup called her friend Detective Larry Gaines.

"Morning, counselor," Detective Gaines said.

"Hi Larry, off the record?"

"Always. How can I help you?"

"If I want to trace a print and don't want anyone to know it's me tracing it …?"

"How soon do you need it?"

"Whenever."

"I'm with forensics, now is not a good time."

"You at a scene?"

"A murder. This may take a couple hours. Can I get back to you when I'm out of here?"

"Sure. Who got murdered?"

"Looks like an out-of-towner. Texas plates. Fancy Porsche."

Lily Cup stood and stepped into a corner of the kitchen, muffling her voice.

"How'd he die?"

"Bludgeoned."

"Ouch."

"Head. Coroner thought brain hemorrhaging caused death. Blow to the head. Robbery. I'm not buying it yet, the robbery thing."

"What's it looking like to you?"

"Cold-blooded murder."

"A contract killing? A hit?"

"I don't know about that, but whoever did it knew what they were doing."

"How so?"

"The victim was sitting in his car with one blow right between his eyes that killed him instantly. No broken glass, no sign of struggle. This was a professional kill."

"Think it was a gang hit?" Lily Cup asked.

"Well will you lookie' here," Larry said.

"What?"

"I know it wasn't robbery now," Larry said.

"How's that?"

"I just pulled a roll of $1,800 from his pants side pocket. And here we have a wallet with all his cards in his other pocket."

"When did this happen?"

"First guess— about one a.m."

"Can you tell me the plate?"

"It's evidence, I can't."

"I'm not going to do anything with it, Larry, just curious if its personalized."

Detective Gaines told her the plate number.

"Thanks Larry. Call me later."

Lily Cup texted the plate number to herself and went back to the table.

"My guy can track prints," Lily Cup said.

"Good," Peck said.

"Where were we?" Lily Cup asked.

"I have to figure a way to get inside," Peck said.

"What do you mean, inside?"

"To see how they work, to find her," Peck said.

"Are we still talking about saving a girl?"

"Ah *oui*."

"Sounds like you want to bust up their operations."

"Why not, cher?"

"You can't be serious."

"Why not?"

"They'll find you out and kill you. That's why not."

"I have ideas."

"That's what scares me."

"Today I go see some people, cher. Where will you be later?"

"I thought we were in this together, Peck."

"Ah *oui*, cher. Let me do some trackin'. Where will you be later?"

"You want to go to Charlie's and dance?"

"Nah nah, not tonight."

"I'll be here, then."

"Can I stay again, cher?"

"Sure. I'll cook," Lily Cup said.

Peck's phone rang.

"Hey pretty Millie, how you are?"

"You turned your phone off. I don't like when you turn your phone off," Millie said.

"Ah, so sorry, sweetheart—I'm investigating for Lily Cup. It was all night. Storyville, the Quarter, all over, bébé."

"Are you still investigating?"

"Ah *oui*. Four, maybe three more days. How you are, bébé?"

"I haven't started my paper and I've got exams all week next week. I should be studying. I miss you so much."

"It'll be soon, bébé. Tell Peck when you're coming so I can tell Lily Cup."

"I love you, Peck. If you have to turn your phone off text me first so I know, and I don't worry."

"Love you."

"I love you too. Bye."

Peck went upstairs and hid the plastic freezer bag holding Lauren's handbag with the fingerprints on it. He came back downstairs.

"Peck, so much you're not telling. I thought—"

"Cher, what did you tell me to do yesterday?"

"What do you mean?"

"What was Peck supposed to do?"

"Run and observe."

"Well, I can't run and observe without seein' things. So how about me see the things and you help me understand them?"

"Shit," Lily Cup groaned.

"Now what's the matter, cher?"

"I feel like I've been scolded by my teacher."

"See you later," Peck said as he left the house.

10.

PECK PARKED DOWN THE STREET from the shotgun house. He walked to it and let himself in. Gabe was in his recliner sipping coffee and reading a morning newspaper. Peck poured a cup, went in and sat next to Gabe.

"Well, hello, my brother."

Peck was all business.

"Gabe when you were in the army, did you do—how you say—undercover work?"

"Many times, son. It was part of my job. Went with the territory."

"Were you good at it, Gabe?"

"Son, a black man in America had to learn stealth at an early age just to survive. If taught right, a black man knows that it's safest to go through life trying not to be seen. I was the best at it."

"You want to help me, Gabe?"

"In a heartbeat, my brother."

"How you say, top secret?"

"Of course. Just you and me, son."

"No questions, Gabe?"

"I'm good with being on a need-to-know basis, my brother."

"Gabe, what's the best way to investigate, like if— say you had a team working for you?"

"I'd assign each member one task, only one thing to do."

"Hanh?"

"Only one objective—one target, son. That gets the best result. If you give someone two objectives, he always has one of them as a reason to fail, one excuse. One objective and there are no excuses."

"Gabe, get in my pickup, ol' man. We go for a ride."

Gabe stood and took his coffee cup into the kitchen and placed it on the counter.

"I'll explain on the way," Peck said. "I need your idea about something and maybe can learn from you."

Gabe donned his cap, selected a walking stick and stepped outside. Peck pushed buttons, starting the pickup. They walked to it, climbed in and drove off.

"Lily Cup told me what that police detective said about working with you, Gabe, when they charged you with murdering that man."

"Remind me, son."

"About the man you conked, Gabe?"

"No, remind me what the detective said."

"Lily Cup say that detective told the judge that because you were a black man and because he, the detective, was a black man too, you understood each other better."

"I remember—the lieutenant detective Larry Gaines, a brother. Yes, that's right. That's what the man said … and it was the truth. Our culture, our shared life experiences being black in America lets us understand our vernacular, where we're coming from."

"He's a good frien' of Lily Cup."

"I've heard. They went to school together," Gabe said. "He got me off those murder charges last year by taking the time to find the weapon used to attack me. He found it after forensics stopped looking."

"He's a good tracker, this Lieutenant Larry?"

"He's the best," Gabe said.

Peck turned on Canal Street and followed slow traffic to a parking garage. He parked and they climbed out. Peck searched his iPhone for a definition of the word *vernacular*.

"What's that under your seat?" Gabe asked.

Peck looked over.

"An umbrella," Peck said.

"It's a beauty," Gabe said. "Is it bronze?"

"Lily Cup gave it to me. It was her daddy's. Umbrella inside the cane. Let's go into the hotel, we'll get coffee. I explain better with coffee."

Coffee and beignets were served.

"Gabe, do army guys know what concierge is?"

"Of course, we do."

"Like ever'thing what they do, concierge people?"

"Are you asking me to test me or are you asking me because you don't know what they do, son?"

"I don't know what they do," Peck said.

"Ignorance isn't a crime, son. You don't know what a concierge is?"

"Nah nah."

"How would you even know about them then?"

"Gabe, I walk in and out of fourteen hotels on Canal Street and ever' one of them hotels had a man or lady in front standing up at a table or sitting down at a desk with a sign what say *concierge*. That's how ... and I looked *concierge* up in my dictionary."

"Son, a concierge is important. They may not be the heartbeat of a fine hotel like this one here, but they are the pulse. They know hotel guests by first names, where they're from and what they like. They know the city better than anyone. They know where to get theatre tickets for sold-out performances, how to get a table at a packed restaurant, how to place a bet at a track somewhere."

"How about sex, Gabe?"

"I see where you're going with this, son."

Peck leaned in and whispered.

"Sex, Gabe?"

"My guess is these people work a long time and hard to get where they are and they respect their positions. I can't see them taking risks hustling sex. They do see everything though, and may know what's going on or who to call."

"Ah."

"It's a delicate issue, son, sex, but I'm guessing if they don't know who to call, or don't make the call, they'll likely know someone who does know."

"Big money tips, I'm thinking," Peck said.

"Lots of cash changes hands for favors," Gabe said.

"Dass for true."

"Here's where we start, Gabe." Peck nodded toward the concierge desk in the lobby. "At that concierge."

"Sex for money is all over the city, Peck, not just in some hotels."

"One target, one objective—your words, Captain," Peck said. "We gonna' start with hotels."

"Peck, on the ride over you talked about cultures communicating one-on-one with each other—about how a black police detective and I understood each other. This day you started asking how cultures communicate better among their own."

"Ah *oui*."

"What's culture got to do with a concierge knowing about some out-of-towner getting laid?"

"You're a black man, Gabe. I'm Cajun French."

"Where're you going with this, son?"

"I have an idea, is all. I learned it from hearing about that lieutenant man Larry, who got you out of that murder trouble you was in."

"I'm here, my brother."

"You and me have to find which concierges are black or Creole, and which are Acadian or Cajun French."

"What if they're neither?" Gabe asked.

"Then we don't talk to them," Peck said.

"I'm listening, son."

"Gabe you talk with the black and Creole concierges, and I talk with the Cajun and the Acadian French ones."

"You're thinking like an eagle, son," Gabe said. "A brother will always open up to another brother."

"Same for fishers, Gabe. Same thing. Cajuns will talk, don't you know?"

"But what are we talking to them about, son?"

"That's secret until I figure out what I need, Gabe."

"I see," Gabe said. "You're tracking right now, aren't you, son?"

"Ah *oui*. Help me ol' man? No matter what?"

"My brother. No matter what."

"You and me Gabe, no Lily Cup's ears, no Sasha's."

"My lips are sealed, son. Top secret."

"Thanks, frien'."

"This still about that girl you saw?"

"Ah *oui*. Other sex slaves too, Gabe, dass for true."

"You be careful, son. You be very careful."

"I promise, Gabe. Got you some army advice?"

"I do. Know who you're talking to before you open your mouth. Be careful about looking at someone too long. As sure as I'm sitting here, too long of a glance or the wrong question to the wrong person, and some'll turn in a heartbeat if they think there's money in it for themselves."

"We'll make sure we only talk to right ones, Gabe. I got an idea, Captain."

Gabe smiled at Peck's use of "we." He rubbed his face generously with both hands while anxiously grinning into his palms, like it was Christmas morning, waiting to hear what Peck's eagle brain and eyes have already thought up as a way to qualify certain *talkers* as the right and safe ones to talk to. He had a glimmer in his eyes, as if he wished he could time-travel back to his early military career days in Korea and in Vietnam, and he could take Peck with him. He reached for a beignet and waited for Peck to speak.

"That's why I brought you here, Gabe."

"Talk to me, son."

"First thing, Gabe. You and me have to find out if the concierge we might be thinkin' of gettin' with is a father or a mother."

"Sumbitch. That's perfect."

"We ax to see pics of the kids. That'd be a start, dass for true."

"And if he's a father or she's a mother they're not approving young kids as sex slaves. They'll be thinking of their own kids," Gabe said.

"Looking at pictures of their own kids while showin' them to us will remind them, Gabe."

"That's smart, son. Parents are less likely to arrange sex."

"And we ain't lookin' for the bad ones, Gabe. We looking for the good ones."

"Brilliant, son."

"You say your own self, Gabe. The concierge is the pulse of a hotel. They see and know ever'thing. They may not get sex for somebody, but they always know what's goin' on, especially if somebody else does."

"Perfect!" Gabe said.

"Ya think, Gabe?"

"When do we start, son?"

"I need to see some things first, and then maybe I can tell you better what we talkin' with them about. Later, I be ready. Maybe tomorrow, Captain. I need to think on it."

"Just give me the word."

"Thanks, frien'."

"Will I see you tonight, son?"

"Nah nah, not tonight. Tomorrow maybe."

11.

PECK KNEW HE HAD TO come up with a secret way of communicating with André without being traced. He dropped Gabe off and headed to the French Quarter. Driving on Canal Street he saw a phone store, found a place to park and went in.

"Do you have any particular phone in mind, sir, or are you just looking?" a clerk asked.

"*Je ne sais pas sur les téléphones,*" Peck said. ("I don't know about telephones.")

"Sir, do you speak English?"

"*Je suis désolé non. Français s'il vous plaît?*" ("I'm sorry no. French please?")

"Just a minute, sir."

The sales clerk stepped away and spoke with someone. A female clerk approached Peck with a smile.

"*Puis-je vous aider, monsieur?*" ("Can I help you, sir?")

"*Français cajun, cher?*" ("Cajun French, cher?")

"*Je suis. J'ai grandi à Pointe-de-l'Église, toi?*" ("I am. I grew up in Church Point, you?")

"Carencro, cher."

"*Vous ne parlez pas anglais?*" the girl asked. ("You don't speak English?")

"*Cher, je ne veux pas hacher des questions stupides à un vendeur. Cajun, j'ai confiance.*" ("Cher, I don't want to ask dumb questions to some salesman. Cajun I trust.")

"I understand. So, you grew up in Carencro?"

"Ah *oui.*"

"We were neighbors then," the girl whispered. "We can talk quietly. How can I help my Cajun friend?"

"I got me a frien', cher. I want to give a phone to him."

"You a good frien', bébé."

"I don't want to pay regular, cher, how you say, more than one time. You have phones like that?"

"You mean a phone with no monthly payments?"

"Ah *oui*."

"We have prepaid phones. You buy one and you pay what you like for minutes or time when you buy it. Whoever you give the phone to can use it free until the minutes run out. Your friend will have to buy more minutes on it when it runs out, if he wants more time."

"Can I ax you like whose name is on the phone?"

"Nobody's. Sometimes people use them for a while and just throw them away when the time is used up."

"Does it have a number and can it text and all?"

"Prepaid phones will do everything any phone will do. It's just an inexpensive phone."

"Thanks, cher."

"No problem."

"Can I go figure how many phones and come back later, maybe tomorrow?"

"Sure."

"You won't think I'm crazy, cher?"

"We Cajuns crazy. You pass a good time and I see you when I see you."

"What days you work, cher? I'll wait for you."

"Here every day. I'm Aurelie. Just ask for me."

"Dass for true. I promise."

"What's your name?"

"Peck, cher. Well, Boudreaux, but Peck is good."

Aurelie walked Peck outside, and watched him walk away after a friendly wave.

12.

PECK WALKED FROM THE PHONE STORE to Bourbon Street a few blocks into the Quarter. He didn't see Lauren and her pedicab. He turned around and walked back to his pickup. There was one important detail on his mind in the tracking mode. He drove home to talk with Gabe about the black Mercedes parked on its rims in Metairie two days ago.

"Gabe, I got to find out who owns that car, jes' in case."

"In case of what, son."

"In case it's the same car pimp man shoved the slave girl into. If I find who owns it, I maybe could find the pimp, the girl maybe. Gabe, I need your help, and I have an idea."

"How can I help?"

"Somebody took it, Gabe. The car was gone. Not in front of the bookstore today."

"Probably towed," Gabe said.

"If a car was left on the street like that and they—how you say—towed it, where they take it?"

"Every city has an auto pound, son. If it got towed my guess is it's in the pound."

Peck searched his phone—New Orleans auto pound.

"Ah *oui*. Here it is. I found it. I'm going there to look around. I'll be right back."

Peck jumped up and headed for the door.

"You be careful, son."

Peck set his GPS and followed directions to the auto pound on Claiborne Avenue. At the destination he turned in and pulled through the wrought iron gate and wire mesh fencing. A husky black man stepped out of a shed and approached. Peck saw him, stopped and opened his window and shouted out.

"Sorry, mister. I'll have to come back. I forgot to bring me somethin'. I be right back."

The man flipped a friendly wave, turned and headed back as Peck drove off, went home and got Gabe.

"I just went to the pound. The man that come out was a black man, Gabe."

"What's the problem, son?"

"It's that culture thing. I got to get this right."

"My brother," Gabe said with a grin.

"The second I saw him I think of the culture thing and told him I forgot something and would be back. That's why I came for you."

"Gotcha, son. Let's go."

Peck explained to Gabe that he'd tell him just enough about the Mercedes to be believable, but not so much to make it look like Gabe was undercover, snooping and maybe draw suspicion. They agreed that Gabe would do the talking and Peck would stay in the pickup. As they pulled past the New Orleans Auto Pound sign, Gabe opened his door, got out and with his cane walked toward the husky black man, who stepped out of the office shed and waited on its top step.

"My brother," Gabe said.

He held his fist out for a pump. "Gabe."

"What's by you, brother Gabe?" the auto pound man asked. "Damon."

"Just an old veteran brother gettin' by on military pension. Looking for deals."

"This brother saw Iraq. How can I help you?"

"You saw Iraq? Did you know a Private Jordan?"

"Can't say I did, brother. Can't say."

"My boy. A good boy. Lost him there. Friendly fire."

"My brother."

"Damon do these cars ever find their rightful owners, or can a brother get him a good deal at a car auction?"

"Depends."

"Always a catch for folks watching pennies," Gabe said.

"If the owner pays up, they can come get their car out, but after ninety days it's sold."

"Could a brother get in line for one of the sales?"

"Depends on the car."

"I have one in mind, but I don't see it," Gabe said.

"Owner likely picked it up."

"Any way of checking and finding out, my brother?"

"You'll have to ask my boss."

"Is he here?"

"He's here. I'll go ask."

"My brother."

"Brother knows they have their ways," Damon said to Gabe while he walked toward his office shed. "I know they sell to wholesalers—to auctions. They have ways."

"I saw a Mercedes on rims over in Metairie, can you find out if that car is here?"

"When'd you see it?"

"Sunday, Monday, I don't remember. My memory ain't what it used to be."

"I hear that. Let me ask. What color was it?"

"Black."

Damon stepped into the office and left the door open. Gabe looked through the fencing at cars as if he was window shopping. In time Damon came out with a manager.

"Mercedes, who's askin'?" the manager asked.

"Over here, it was me," Gabe said.

"Who's askin'?" the manager repeated.

"Just an old vet looking for a deal."

"That Mercedes is locked up. Impounded. What's your interest in it?"

"Me and a friend rode by it, and it looked pretty clean. Shape of it I thought it might be getting towed. On its rims. Just wondering if it's been towed and going to be sold, is all. Sister needs a good set of wheels," Gabe said.

"Some kind of a murder investigation going on. That car is evidence. It's locked up, sorry."

"Do you ever sell any of these cars?"

"We sell some cars, but that one's not for sale."

"Thank you for your time," Gabe said.

The manager turned and went into the office shed.

"Sorry, brother," Damon said.

"Where do they lock up cars they're investigating?"

"They don't tell me."

"Thank you, my brother."

"A brother might check the car dealer in Metairie."

"The car dealership?" Gabe asks.

"You say it was parked in front of a bookstore, in Metairie?"

"Veterans Boulevard."

"That's the one, brother. I take my little girls to that book store. It's next door to a car dealership."

"Fancy cars?"

"Brother might check there, is all."

Gabe fist-pumped Damon, turned and got in the pickup. Peck backed around and pulled out.

"We're going to Metairie, son."

"Why Metairie, Gabe?"

"Your car is at a dealership next to the bookstore."

"You're goin' home ol' man. You did good."

13.

PECK TOOK THE METAIRIE EXIT and turned onto Veterans Boulevard and slowed his pickup to a stealth crawl, looking for any telltale signs of the abandoned car. It was nowhere in sight. He parked two blocks from the bookstore and around the corner of the car dealership. He walked around and in the driveway behind the dealership through its service entrance and up to a service desk.

"Can I help you?" the service manager asked.

"I'm looking for—how you say—a car you might have here and to see if you want to sell it," Peck said.

"You'll want sales, sir. They're through that door over there. Go to the showroom."

"Nah nah, frien', this car may be wrecked or towed and you have it."

"What car?"

"Black Mercedes."

"We have a lot of black Mercedes."

"This one didn't have no tires settin' on Veterans Boulevard in front of the bookstore Monday."

"On its rims?"

"Dass for true, frien'. No tires."

The service manager pulled a drawer with tabbed files. He thumbed through a dozen or more files, pulled a job ticket out and read it to himself. His lips mouth read a whisper, "On rims, needs lift tow, Veterans Boulevard—NOLA PD."

"We have it," the service manager said.

"Ah, good."

"I don't think it's for sale, though."

"Can I maybe look at it, to see if it's the same car?"

"I'll have to ask. Wait here."

"Thanks, frien'."

The service manager set the job ticket down on the lower desk from the service counter, turned and walked away. Feigning reading emails on his iPhone, Peck snapped pictures of the inverted job ticket. The service man came back.

"That car's not available."

"Can I look at it?"

"Sorry. If you want a car, new or pre-owned, you'll have to go through that door and talk to sales. They can help you."

"Thanks, frien'."

Peck left the dealership and walked to his pickup, starting it within sight. He placed a call to Millie.

"I was just thinking of you," Millie said. "And here you are."

"I love you, Millie."

"I love you too. Where are you?"

"Can I ax something important?"

"Of course, silly."

"Remember when we went to the library place when we went to Knoxville, cher?"

"How could I forget that library? That was where we were when I knew I was head over heels madly in love with you," Millie said.

"Remember you found on that computer where knife man lived from his motorcycle license plate?"

"Yes! That was so exciting. I remember."

"I need you to find me something now, Millie, but it's secret and you can't text me, unless you know I have the phone in my hand, cher. I don't want anybody reading texts about what I'm axin'. Understand?"

"I understand."

"If you find something you text me you ready, only that, cher."

"If I find something I only text '*I'm ready*'?"

"Ah *oui*. Then you have to wait. I text you a code word so you know I have the phone in my hand. This is so secret you don't tell. Not Lily Cup, not Gabe, nobody, cher."

"Just like Knoxville," Millie said.

"Ah *oui*."

"What's the code, Peck?"

"You pick a word, cher. That way you'll remember."

"*William.*"

"William, cher!? For true?"

"You told me to pick a word, Peck. It's *William.*"

"You are so bad, cher."

"When I text you 'I'm ready', I'll wait for you to text me back, *William.* That way I'll know it's safe to text you."

Peck grinned.

"Okay, okay, code is *William.* You got a pen?"

"Yes."

"Write this down, cher."

Peck read the car's Vehicle Identification Number to Millie from the picture of the job ticket. Millie repeated it back to him.

"That's an awfully long license plate," Millie said. "Are you sure—?"

"Nah, nah, it's a *vehicle identification number,* cher. It's like a brand on the engine of a car. That number will tell us who owns the car and where they live."

"I'm glad I asked. What did you call it?"

"Vehicle identification number, cher."

"Okay, got it. I have classes all day but I can do it tonight. I'm going to be at the library studying."

"Thanks sweet Millie."

"What do you need me to find out?"

"Owner man's name. Address, maybe."

"Is he a bad man?"

"Dass for true, cher. Very bad man."

"What did he do?"

"He kidnapped and raped a nine-year-old girl and he pimped her to old men. He's a bad man, bébé."

"Pimp? You mean he makes her be a prostitute?"

"Ah *oui.*"

"In New Orleans?"

"Ah *oui.*"

"How do you even know him, Peck?"

"I saw him beat her up when I was cleaning Lily Cup's offices. I saw it out the window."

"A time to be born and a time to die," Millie whispered into the phone. *"A time to kill and a time to heal."*

"Millie, I love you so much. I love you forever."

"Ecclesiastes," Millie said. "Save that little girl, Peck. You have to save her."

"I promise, cher. Our secret always."

"If he has one little girl, he has others, Peck."

"Dass for true, bébé. Sex trafficking. The girls get slaved forever. We got to help them."

"I love you so much Boudreaux Clemont Finch."

"I love you, Millie, Peck's every thought. Help me find who owns that car."

"I'm going to cry. Bye."

Peck drove home to get some clothes before going to Lily Cup's.

"Any luck, son?"

"I found the car."

"The same car?"

"Same car, Captain."

"You are amazing. What's your next move, son?"

Peck didn't answer.

"How about Charlie's tonight, Peck? Jazz, a bowl of red beans, some relaxation?"

"I'll be back and drive you there, Gabe, but can I tell you later if I'm goin' to stay and dance? I'm waiting for something. If I get what I need, I can't stay at Charlie's."

Gabe was good with that.

14.

PECK CAME UP WITH A COMMUNICATION PLAN for André. He parked and stepped into the phone store, looking for Aurelie. He caught her eye. She was with a customer. She raised a finger signaling for Peck to wait, that she wouldn't be long. He sat on a bench, watching people. Aurelie walked over.

"Hey, Carencro. You doin' good, bébé?"

"How you are, cher? You lookin' so good, dass for true."

"Did you decide on a phone, Peck?" Aurelie asked.

"I did, cher. Can we talk a spell now?"

"Sure."

They found a sales table by a window.

"What'd you decide, bébé?" Aurelie asked.

"Cher, if I buy three of these—how you say—prepaid phones and I put three-hundred dollars on each of them, would that last them a time?"

"Yeah, three hundred would be good."

"How about if all they did was text?"

"The phones would last a real long time."

"You sell a lot of these phones like this, cher?"

"The guys sell more prepaids, but I sell some, sure."

"Why do the guys sell more?"

"I guess some people don't want a girl snooping in their business. Who knows?"

"What kind of people buy these, cher?"

"All kinds. Parents buy them for kids who lose things all the time. Sometimes girls buy them when they're cheating. Ha ha, I've seen that too."

"For true?"

Aurelie leaned in with a whisper.

"There's this one married lady? She brought a young dude here. She gave him one, and she got one for herself."

"How much younger, cher?"

"Like she was maybe fifty, and he looked twenty. She was beautiful, though."

"Aurelie, you got you a young—how you say—boy like that with a phone, cher?" Peck quipped with a guffaw.

"I wish. No, I'm just boring me, work, work."

"Jolie fille comme toi, les hommes feraient la queue pour toi, cher." ("Pretty girl like you, men would line up for you, cher.")

"Tu me taquines. Je connais des garçons. Quelques. Personne de spécial cependant." ("You're teasing me. I know boys. Some. Nobody special though.")

"Do you dance, cher?"

"Are you going to buy a phone? I don't want to get in trouble talking too much."

Peck pulled a thousand dollars in twenties from his pocket and handed them to Aurelie.

"Give me three phones and use all this to make them good. Okay cher?"

"Tax and everything and the rest in time?"

"Ah *oui*, cher. Do your thing."

"I'll go get them. Don't you want to use a credit card for record keeping?"

"Use the cash."

"No problem … and yes, I dance."

"Dass so good, cher. Jazz or you do that Zydeco?"

"Dixieland and Zydeco, I'm pretty good. I'd like to try jazz, though."

"Cher, can I ax somethin' personal?"

"Well, that depends. How personal?"

"You ever get pimps or girls, you know, what come get phones like these?"

"That's not personal. Yeah. I do."

"You want to dance jazz with me sometime, cher?"

"Depends."

"On what?"

"Are you cheating on someone?"

"Nah, nah."

"You're not a pimp, are you?"

"Ha ha! I have a girlfriend I love more than anything else, cher. She's in Texas at university. I can dance, she say I can dance good, it's okay. You'd like Charlie's."

"Where's Charlie's?"

"Frenchmen Street. Charlie's Blue Note. It's jazz."

"Maybe me and a girlfriend will try it."

Peck hands Aurelie his iPhone.

"Take my number, cher. Text me if you want to dance."

"All right."

She noted his number in her phone.

"Some good beans and rice, cher, not expensive like the Quarter," Peck said.

"Let me go get your phones. I'll get them turned on."

"Thanks, cher."

15.

PECK LIKED HIS PROGRESS as a tracker, but it was in his nature to avoid overconfidence. His conscience could only reflect the end game, the purpose of the mission he was on. It was about children being bought and sold—slaved.

He was fueled by his own childhood. When he ran away at nine, he was left for dead … likely eaten by an alligator. He wasn't sexually abused, but his mother was raped, and he was slaved. In his mind what he needed was the approval of the only man who knew the story of Mémé's insanity, of Peck's mother's rape and of his biological father's ultimate demise. The man who knew the secrets to Peck's childhood was Mr. Hebert, who ran a bank in Killian. Mr. Hebert learned the story of Peck and his mother from his lifetime best friend and fishing companion, Dr. Pontelbon.

Dr. Pontelbon died years back but he left personal letters for Mr. Hebert to read. Letters Dr. Pontelbon wanted Peck to read if he was ever found alive. Peck left New Orleans and drove the hours it took to get to visit Mr. Hebert in Killian. Peck needed affirmation that his mission was the right path. Peck's phone rang. Peck pressed the Bluetooth button.

"How you are, cher?"

"Where are you, Peck?" Lily Cup asked.

"Drivin' someplace, cher."

"We need to talk."

"Okay."

"We can't talk here. Meet me at Charlie's tonight?"

"You have court tomorrow?"

"I do."

"You want me in court, cher? You got work for me?"

"Yes, but no talking about you-know-what in court."

"I understand."

"Charlie's tonight?"

"How about your house, cher?"

"Even better."

"Cher, I'm going someplace now but I'll be back. Let me drive Gabe to Charlie's later so he can dance. We'll wait for Sasha and after she gets there, I go to your house. Captain say she's coming to dance. She'll take him home, so I'll come to your place."

"Will you eat at Charlie's or should I cook?"

"Nah nah, you cook. We'll pass a good time, cher."

"I'll get a bowl of crawfish and some oysters."

"Aye-yi-yi, we'll pinch the tail and suck the head, cher. I'll shuck oysters if you get them. We can talk all night, maybe."

"Text me when you leave Charlie's," Lily Cup said.

"*Au revoir*, cher."

16.

PECK PULLED INTO KILLIAN and found a parking spot on the town square. He walked into the bank and found Mr. Hebert shaking a man's hand before turning into his office when he caught Peck's eye.

"Well, well, well, Mr. Boudreaux Clemont Finch, if you're not a sight for these tired old eyes," Mr. Hebert said. "Come in, son, come in. What brings you to Killian?"

"Hey hey, Mr. Hebert, I come to visit and to have some of your good coffee, dass for true."

"Our 'good coffee' has been coming from the coffee shop up the street nigh on ten years now, but we can arrange some, sure enough. Have a seat, son. It's so good to see you."

Mr. Hebert picked up his phone and asked the bank's receptionist to make a coffee run.

"Constance asks about you and that pretty girl Millie all the time, Peck. How is Millie and how's your momma?"

"Millie is good, Mr. Hebert. Mamma is so good too. I saw her a couple days ago. One more year at Baylor for Millie and then she be with me and Gabe in New Or-lee-anh. I'm working and studying hard at Tulane, dass for true."

"Always a pleasure to see you, young man, but a man that busy must have a big reason for coming all this way just to see me. What's on your mind, son?"

"Mr. Hebert, can I ax you about my father again?"

Mr. Hebert rested back with troubled eyes.

"What about your father, son?"

"Mr. Hebert, Gabe says I can't call him my daddy, cause he raped mamma, but can you tell me about him again, Mr. Hebert, so I can hear it again?"

"Just what would you like me to tell you, son?"

"Jes' tell me the story again, Mr. Hebert. Please?"

Mr. Hebert pulled his desk drawer open and lifted a manila envelope from it.

"Interesting you should ask, Peck. Every so often I'll read my best friend's letter— my copy of the doc's letter to you. I think about him often. Old friends do that, son. He was dead five years when you first read it. I keep my copy of it here in this drawer, and I'll pull it out now and again just to say hello to the memory of my old friend. It's always here in this drawer. Reading it brings the doc alive and in the room with me."

"Mr. Hebert, can I hear the part in the letter when they went fishing?"

As Mr. Hebert scanned the letter with his eyes, the receptionist brought in coffees.

"I found that part, son. Are you ready?"

Peck nodded. Mr. Hebert began reading.

"Two things you need to know Mr. Finch. The first, my friend, Hal, is about to read you. The other is something special for you in the second envelope.

The first happened two years after you were born, Mr. Finch. Mr. Devine and I planned a day of fishing. Before he got to the lake, I packed my end of the boat with a thermos of lemonade, my small ice cooler with sandwiches, and a paper sack with two bags of potato chips. I rolled my yellow slicker around my shotgun in case I saw a low-flying duck. It wasn't legal, but the thought of duck for dinner crossed most fishers' minds and most law would turn a blind eye on a single duck. Devine eventually showed. He packed his end of the boat with a small cooler, some beer, and a hoagie sandwich. I backed the boat into the lake and then parked my car and trailer before we headed out on the Maurepas. We went to the middle of the lake for the bigger bass. "

Peck interrupted.

"Mr. Hebert, can I ax you something before you read more, please?"

"Of course, son. If I know the answer, I'll tell you."

"Mr. Hebert, this Mr. Devine man what was my father, didn't he rape other women at that hospital? Like didn't he rape more than jes' my mamma?"

"He raped three women that we know of for certain. It could have been more. He impregnated two of them. One of the women died in childbirth. She was twenty-two. One was your mamma. He doesn't deserve a 'mister' son and your friend Gabe is correct, he doesn't deserve 'daddy' either. His name was Guillaume Devine, and he was a lowlife alcoholic Creole, came up from the gulf shores after years working on a shrimp boat and getting fired."

"Okay, you can read."

Mr. Hebert continued.

"Mr. Finch, it was after his fourth beer when the man asked me whatever happened to that gal that used to come by. When I asked him who he was referring to, he described your mother. When I told him she still came by to visit her mother he made a comment ... he said he sure would like to get with her. Mr. Finch, I'm not the sort of a man who blurts out without thinking, but for some reason all that came to my mind was to say, 'You're the one, aren't you?' I remember him looking at me, first in surprise, then with a low sneer. 'So, what if I am?' All I remember, Mr. Finch is that I wasn't afraid. I even repeated 'You did it. Three women—or was it more?' Guillaume tossed his sandwich in the lake and began unsnapping his hunting knife. 'You'll never know, old man—and you'll never tell, neither. You're about to get out and swim with the gators.' I remember every word he said. I reached in my slicker and took my shotgun and just that fast I shot him in the face, pumped quickly and shot him again in the chest. He fell overboard and floated face down. I motored back to shore where, off in the distance, I could see him floating. I went directly to the sheriff's office and told him the story. He sent me home and that was more than twenty years ago and he hasn't said a word about it.

"I'm sorry, Mr. Finch. I don't know what came over me that day. I hope you have a good life. Please say hello to your mother. She's a nice lady."

Mr. Hebert set the papers on his desk and dabbed his eyes with a handkerchief. He sipped coffee looking at Peck's eyes.

"Mr. Hebert, Gabe say that he was my father because he raped my mamma, that Devine man, but he was no daddy to me."

"Gabe's a smart man, son, most would agree. Guillaume Devine was an evil man cruelly taking advantage of defenseless, helpless women."

"Mr. Hebert, I read a book, *Grapes of Wrath*, by this John—"

"*The plows crossed and recrossed the rivulet marks*," Mr. Hebert said.

"Hanh?"

"First paragraph, chapter one, Peck. My freshman year in college. I had to stand before my class and read that chapter aloud. I didn't know what *rivulet* meant, and my professor gave me a B."

"Why a B for not knowing *rivulet*, Mr. Hebert? I wouldn't have known it if I didn't look it up."

"Peck, are you telling me you looked it up while you were reading the book?"

"Yes sir. It means water, like a crick or something."

"Well, you're wiser than me, son. My professor gave me a B for not reading it before class and for not looking up words I didn't know."

"But *rivulet* wasn't the important word, *marks* was the important one," Peck said.

"I knew that meant the rivers and streams were dry, only their *marks* remained," Mr. Hebert said.

"Your professor should give you an A, Mr. Hebert. You know the meaning of the whole sentence, just not one word."

"You have a wonderful mind, son. You have a good life ahead."

"Would the man that raped Mamma and the other women, would he rape more women, ya think?"

"Very likely. Defenseless women especially."

"So it's good the doc shot him?"

"I think so. My Constance agrees. Seemed the sheriff agreed too."

"Can I ax you something Mr. Hebert?"

"Anything, son."

"Tom Joad conked a guard under the bridge. Was it right he did that— conk him dead?"

Mr. Hebert sat back and reflected.

"Back in 1934, Peck, over in Bienville Parish up by Sailes?"

"Where's that, Mr. Hebert?"

"Louisiana, up bayou, as you'd say, son."

"Ah *oui*."

"Six armed men set a trap and ambushed and killed Bonnie and Clyde."

"Who was Bonnie and Clyde, Mr. Hebert?"

"They were robbers and killers, son. Cold, ruthless killers. Bonnie and Clyde killed thirteen people. Those times were simpler times in the country, son, and the stores, banks and police feared for their lives. These ruthless people were desperate outlaw killers."

Peck didn't respond.

"They had to be stopped, Peck. Nobody could get close enough to catch them. They killed six or eight police officers alone. They would have killed more. One man tracked them, son."

"One man?"

"One man, Peck. Texas Ranger—Francis Hammer."

Peck listened like a schoolboy.

"They counted fifty-five bullets in their bodies, son."

"Aye-yi-yi."

"Bonnie was twenty-three, Clyde was twenty-five."

"Mr. Hebert if somebody is bad, like maybe you saw him rape a little girl and he can't be caught, maybe a conk?"

"I'd conk him in a heartbeat, no questions asked, son. I'd conk him sure."

"Thanks for the coffee, Mr. Hebert. Say hello to that pretty lady from me and Millie, please."

"Always good to see you, Boudreaux Clemont."
"Thanks for helping me, frien'."
"Come see us and bring Millie and your momma."

17.

PECK RETURNED TO NEW ORLEANS and parked near the shotgun house.

"Gabe, can we talk before I take you to Charlie's?"

"Anytime, my brother."

They settled in the living room.

"When you did—how you say—investigative work, what's first?" Peck asked.

"We called it reconnaissance, son."

"Hanh?"

"Reconnaissance. We'd get the lay of the land so we could better plan a strategy. We'd have a war room with maps and a bulletin board— the whole megillah."

"You and me going to do the—how you say—*recon* but our war room is our brains, Captain, not anywhere else. Can't nobody ever know what we do."

"I understand."

"Gabe, while I'm doin' some things I have to do, can you go did Canal Street and the Quarter, how you say, recon, recon…"

"Reconnaissance, son?"

"Reconnaissance," Peck said.

"Just what am I looking for, son?"

"You find the hotels where the concierges are black and the hotels where they're Cajun French, like we talked. Make a list in your head and then we go to work this week."

"Give me a couple days, son. You need names?"

"Only names we need are Gabe's concierge or Peck's concierge."

"You dancing tonight, Peck, or you working?"

"I'm taking you to Charlie's and when Sasha gets there I'll go to work."

"Just be careful, son. Be extra careful."

It started to rain when Peck drove Gabe to Charlie's Blue Note. He found a spot and parked. He was hesitant about reaching for the bronze cane with the umbrella inside.

“We okay without an umbrella, Gabe?”

“We’ll be fine, son. Let’s go.”

Gabe and Peck could hear music while they walked into the alley off Frenchman Street. Charlie’s was packed. The dance floor alive with rolling, swaying body motions to soft, smooth jazz and velvety tones of a saxophone, promising a path through heartache. Gabe’s table had a reserved sign on it and the four chairs were inverted and rested on its top.

Gabe caught Charlie’s eye and gave a military salute to him as a thank-you for saving the table. He motioned for Peck to go sit. He’d be back after a visit to the men’s room. Peck looked around the room. André was sitting at the bar, talking to another man in a suit. Peck stood in the crowd, watching André’s reflection in the mirror. It was a few minutes when André caught his eye. Peck motioned his head toward the men’s room. André gestured that he understood. Just as Peck got to the men’s room door, Gabe came out.

“I got to pee, Captain,” Peck said.

“You want beans, son?”

“Nah nah. I’m not staying. Order you a bowl, Gabe, I’ll bring it to the table.”

Gabe stepped over to the window, ordered his bowl and walked to his table by the band. In a few minutes André went into the men’s room, where Peck was waiting.

“You’ve been doing some good tracking, bébé?” André asked. “I see it in your eyes.”

Peck handed him one of the cell phones.

“Mr. André, put this in your pocket.”

André slipped the phone into his pants pocket.

“It’s a prepaid phone I bought from a Cajun French girl I know at a store. It can’t be traced. I trust her, and she told me to pay cash, so ain’t no trace to me possible either.”

“I’m listening, son.”

“Mr. André, if the phone rings, it’s a mistake, don’t answer. Never answer. Nobody knows who has it. My frien’ she turn off the thing inside so it can’t be—how you say—

tracked. If a text comes, you read it, Mr. André, and know that text be good for only maybe a couple hours."

"What texts will I be getting, bébé?"

"Mr. André, you my Godfather, right?"

"I'm honored, son."

"You have to figure the text out your own self, frien', okay? It's safer that way, I think, That way I don't have to lie to anybody, my frien'."

"You really think of me as Godfather, young man?"

"Dass for true, Mr. André, I really do."

André blessed himself with a sign of the cross. He pointed to the men's room door.

"You step out first, son. I'll take a minute, wash my hands."

Gabe was alone at the table.

"No Sasha, Captain?"

"I got you a beer. Sit awhile. She'll be here."

While Peck texted Lily Cup that he was on his way to her house, a girl neither he nor Gabe knew came over to the table and tapped Peck on the shoulder.

"Will you dance with me?" she asked.

Peck shrugged for Gabe's eyes, stood and turned into the girl's arms. They jazz nestled, moved and swayed slowly to a sad trumpet solo—sad sounds. The girl rested her head on his chest as if she knew him, and they turned and slid in step. In a dip to a saxophone's velvety moan, Peck felt his phone vibrate in his pocket. He finished the melancholy dance to a sad jazz song. When it ended the stranger girl lifted her head from his chest.

"Thank you," she said, with tears in her eyes.

"Oh, cher, why so sad?"

"I'll be okay," she said. "Thank you for dancing with me."

Peck watched. The sad girl walked to a table with two other girls and sat down. He pulled the phone from his pocket. It was a text from Millie.

"I'M READY," Millie texted.

"WILLIAM," Peck texted back.

Instantly a return message was texted to him. He read it with a grimace in his eyes. He sat down with Gabe.

"Gabe, that girl was so sad. She was crying. Why she cry like that while dancing?"

"There's sadness in the world, son. When I was a young man, we used to live our lives in a world of families, of dinner tables and of neighbors. We lived in a world of going to church on Sunday and of small kindergarten through twelfth grade school's son. Today's youth, they're anonymous orphans with electronic babysitters, and they're going to schools bigger than small cities. A kid doesn't stand a chance of learning how to talk, much less take care of themselves or survive. They have the whole world's problems in their hands, numbing their brain every day on that stupid thing they hold like it was attached."

Sasha appeared and set her martini down on the table.

"Got room for a lady, boys?"

"Don't even think about sitting down, beautiful lady. Stand at ease."

Sasha offered a sarcastic military salute.

"Aye-aye, Captain."

Gabe stood, pushed his chair in and offered his hand.

"You're exquisite, darling," he said. "Black becomes you like a dream."

"This old thing?" Sasha mused. "I bought this in Memphis traveling with you two vagabonds."

"Ah *oui*." Peck said. "I remember, cher. I danced with you when you wore it first time on—how you say that street?"

"Beale Street?" Sasha asked.

"Beale Street. We danced good that night, I'll say."

"Good memory, Peck. This is the same jumper," Sasha said. "My girls love it. Aren't they marvelous in it?"

"Your girls do the dress proud," Gabe said. "Are we dancing, or are we doing a fashion show?"

Peck bid adieu, stepped out of Charlie's and walked in the rain to his pickup while texting Millie to delete the earlier texts from her phone. A bolt of lightning struck nearby and was followed by a downpour and a tapping on Peck's side window by a key in the hand of a man hidden under an umbrella.

The man lifted and lowered the umbrella quickly, but enough to let Peck know it was André, motioning with his finger for Peck to lower his window.

"André doesn't like surprises, bébé."

"Ah *oui*, Mr. André."

"I need to know, bébé."

"Okay."

"What will be texted?"

Peck looked for prying eyes and ears.

"We're alone," André said.

"Hotel room numbers, Mr. André, and the hotel where trafficking is."

"As it's happening?"

"*Oui*, or goin' to happen, *oui*."

"How reliable?"

"Only people who know for sure— concierges, and they think like us, dass for true and it's reliable for how you say that minute in time. The slave is goin' in or already in the room, for maybe a hour is all."

André disappeared into the rainy New Orleans night.

18.

THE NIGHT WAS RESTLESS clouds and stalking sheets of rain. Pitch black. Peck opened the center console. He lifted out one of the two remaining prepaid phones. He turned it on and waited patiently, watching people on sidewalks covering their heads with newspapers, umbrellas or plastic grocery bags.

The phone was on and it had GPS. He programmed the address Millie had sent him. He proofread it to be certain it matched the address Millie texted. He deleted her text.

The destination was Iberville Street. He saw the word *Storyville* on the screen and his jaw tightened, as if he could hear the red dollar sign tattooed man threatening the girl before slugging her in the stomach and kicking her.

He looked for oncoming cars and pulled onto the street until he came to Simon Bolivar Avenue. His pickup followed that to Loyola Avenue. Peck's eyes were a deadly gray now, and like a seasoned bomber pilot he studied his dash, the RPMs, the fuel tank level, the speed.

A bolt of lightning flashed ahead, and he rolled a knob with his thumb that turned the dash light's brightness down as he turned right on Common Street, then a left on Rampart Street.

He saw the street sign for Iberville Street, pulled to the curb and to a full stop. Was he hesitating or was it his cunning? The young man who has seen a fish reeled in that had been bitten in half. The young man who has seen the lifeless head of a snake falling from the sky, dropped by its Peregrine Falcon executioner.

He knew the things he must do. Being careful was among them. He turned the phone off, returned it to the console, blessed himself and kissed his thumb with an Amen. His pickup crawled left onto Iberville Street. He drove until he saw the house number he was looking for. He passed it, drove to the end of the block, circled under a flash of lightning and returned.

He pulled to a stop several doors away. Another slap of lightning flashed with no sound, but the rain was relentless. There was safety in sheets of rain, Peck knew. Prey can be caught off guard in rain. He reached under the seat and lifted the heavy bronze cane, his gift from Lily Cup.

Peck rested the cane on his lap. He lowered his face into his palms, as if he was praying. He lifted his head, clutched the cane and stepped from the pickup, leaving it running with the lights off.

He walked with determined, quick steps. He wiped his hand on his shirt to get the moisture from it. With a grip on the middle of the cane with his right fist, he rang the doorbell with a fingernail of his left hand. He rang it again.

The sound of a deadbolt and then a door lock turning. The door opened a cautious six inches, and a man's head looked out, as if he was expecting a pizza delivery. Peck saw the red dollar sign tattoo, diamond stud in his ear.

Like a viper, an attacking eel, Peck's left fist reached and clutched the devil man's hair and yanked him through the now open doorway. His clutch of hair never loosened, and in seconds tattoo man was on the sidewalk. In another second his skull was split like a squeezed grape, crushed so fast there was no blood yet.

Like an eel Peck grabbed the phone tattoo man had dropped and slid it into his pocket. Hair leaves no prints, and Peck dashed to the waiting pickup and drove away, the door to the house open. He turned right on Rampart while turning tattoo man's phone off. He jammed it in the console and turned left on Common. He reached behind the seat and lifted a dry T-shirt and towel.

Nearing Lily Cup's house, Peck pulled to the curb and picked up one of his new phones. It was as if he was thinking about calling 911 and reporting the address. Then he likely thought that with a body on the front sidewalk, they will know soon enough. He dropped the phone in his console and drove to Lily Cup's house.

19.

WITH A TALL GLASS OF RYE in her hand, Lily Cup pulled the side kitchen door open.

"Where the hell have you been?" Lily Cup growled.

"With Gabe over at Charlie's, is all."

"Look at you. You're soaking wet."

"Sorry. It's raining, cher."

"You texted you were coming—"

"I know."

Lily Cup looked at her cell.

"That was seventy-two minutes ago."

"Charlie's was filled tonight, cher. Lots of people. Ever' table. You should have seen it. So much noise. A pretty girl with sad eyes axed me to dance, so I danced with her. I had to be polite, cher. She had tears in her eyes."

"Your dancing isn't that bad," Lily Cup quipped. "Come eat crawfish."

The dining room table was topped with newspaper pages and set with sterling silver; Peck's brandy snifter was full.

"At least I got reading done for court," Lily Cup said. "Go put some dry clothes on."

Peck was a hunter and tracker having grown up in the wilds of deadly core swamps filled with snakes, snappers and alligators in Acadiana. He had just killed a man and his instincts likely knew the best way to get through this evening would be to create diversions—distractions. Lily Cup was pouring another rye as Peck came down the stairs in his undershorts and T-shirt.

She smiled. "No commando tonight?"

Peck smiled and sat at the table. In the center was a large sterling silver eggnog punch bowl filled with reddish spiced boiled crawfish. Alongside it was a long pan stacked with raw oysters on shaved ice. They sat and drank their rye and their brandy while Peck shucked oysters and Lily Cup spooned the cocktail sauce. Like playing in the sandbox, they would slide oysters into each other's mouths between sucking on the crawfish tails.

"What's court about tomorrow, cher?"

"Gun problem. Pass the salt, can you reach it?" Lily Cup slurred.

"Murder, cher?"

"Arraignment. Asshole client caught speeding and they find a gun in his car. He's a convicted felon and idiot felons aren't allowed to own or carry. Pash' the Tabasco?"

"Your bottle is half gone. You drunk, cher?"

"Getting that way."

"You okay, cher?"

"Waiting for you."

"Why you need me in court?"

"I don't need you. I want you where I can keep an eye on you. Court won't be a couple hours, but after court you and I are coming here."

"Why here, cher?"

"Here, and you're gonna start tellin' me wha' the fuck you're up to." Lily Cup hiccupped. "No more hidin' shit."

Peck lifted his snifter and Lily Cup lifted her glass, this time for a slurred toast.

"Tomorrow we come here …" Peck started.

Lily Cup hiccupped and interrupted.

"And we bare our shouls …"

"We goin' to get nekked, cher …?"

"Ha!" Lily Cup bellowed.

She stood abruptly, as if it were a dare, pulled her T-shirt up over her head and threw it in Peck's face.

"Why wait 'til tomorrow?" She guffawed.

She unhooked her bra and flung it over her shoulder.

"I love murder," Lily Cup declared, with a weave of her chest.

"Nah nah, cher. Why do you love murder?"

"I get to drink rye. Thas' why I love mourder."

"Cher, you drink rye even …"

"Don't shit there staring."

"Hanh?"

"You can see my tits?"

"Oh my, nice *tetines*, cher. So nice."

"Well, les' see yours."

Peck stood, tore his T-shirt off and tossed it in rags at Lily Cup. He pulled his cotton briefs to the floor, stepped out of them, adjusted his package and sat back down, stark naked. A giggling, bleary-eyed Lily Cup sat with a plop and picked up a crawfish tail, her pinky finger out.

"I think I need sum … coffee," Lily Cup said.

"I'll make it," Peck said, standing up.

Lily Cup smiled at the sight of his William and pointed over her shoulder to the kitchen.

"Thermos," she mumbled.

Peck fetched the thermos and two coffee mugs and sat next to Lily Cup to pour. She slid a filled mug in front of her at the table.

"I'm dis-pointed with you," Lily Cup said.

"Oh, cher, you mad. Why you mad with Peck?"

"Cause you shed' we we're a team and we—well we—oh fuck it." She hiccupped. "You stranded me all alone—you turned your phone off. Where you been all day?"

"Oh, cher, so sorry. I had to go see an old frien', is all. I wanted to talk to an old frien'. Sorry, cher."

"Where …" Lily Cup hiccupped. "Where you going now?"

Peck stood next to her chair and kicked his briefs under the table as she ogled William's waggle. He leaned over to kiss her on the forehead. She wrapped her arms around his neck and as he raised up, she lifted and locked her legs around his waist. He lifted her from her chair.

"I'm going to bed, cher. Long day for Peck, I'll say. Come with me."

As he started up the stairs toward the second-floor landing, Lily Cup whispered into his neck.

"I still got my tights on—"

Before Peck could say a word, she was sound asleep, nestled on his shoulder. He carried her into her room and gently put her on her bed. He pulled her tights off, dropped them to the floor as she rolled into a fetal position. He covered her with a blanket and went to the second bedroom and stretched out on the bed, watched through the window as if he hoped to see a moon on this rainy moonless night. He felt contented. Tiffany was a step closer to freedom.

20.

IN THE CORRIDOR of Orleans District Criminal Court Peck watched a thirtyish man looking at his cell phone. He was a black man, in a dark suit with a green bow tie. Standing next to him was a tall white man with glasses and in a suit and wearing a bow tie. They were obviously waiting for the same court, so Peck approached.

"How you are, frien's?"

The men offered their hands.

"I'm Simon Dermott," the tall one said. This is my associate, Damas Aubrey, good to meet you …and you are?"

Peck shook their hands.

"Boudreaux Finch. You lawyers?"

"I'm a writer, Boudreaux," Simon said. "Damas is my research assistant here in Southern Louisiana."

"He writes books," Damas said.

"Ah yi, books are my favorite things, other than my Millie. I love books. What kind of books do you write, Mr. Dermott?"

"Call me Simon. I've written fiction and nonfiction, and now I'm attempting to cloak a murder mystery from this mystical part of the world's imagination."

"Call me Peck. Are you in court today?"

"We're observing."

"For a book?"

"Maybe."

"I go to night school at Tulane and I just read *Grapes of Wrath*. So good I read it two times, I say."

"It's a classic," Simon said.

"You read it?" Peck asked.

"John Steinbeck was one of America's most talented painters of American history."

"Painter? He was a writer, no?"

"Peck, could you see an image, a picture of what was going on in every paragraph?"

"Ah *oui*. Ever' paragraph. Ever' page," Peck said.

"That's painting, my friend. John Steinbeck was the Rembrandt of the written word. His pallet of oils were metaphors, thoughts, images, looks into people's souls. His canvas was the reader's imagination."

"Simon, can I ax you something about that book?"

"Anything."

"Remember Tom Joad?"

"His persona in that novel was iconic, Peck—and when Henry Fonda played Tom Joad in that glorious film account, he became a legend."

"Film?" Peck asked.

"They made a movie of the book. It's an old film now, in black and white, but it's a classic. Watch it sometime. You'll enjoy it."

"Are you an old man, Simon?"

"Good Lord," Simon said.

"I have my reason for axin'," Peck said.

"I was twenty-seven when Mr. Steinbeck passed on, Peck. Does that answer your question?"

"Aye-yi-yi!"

"*Aye-yi-yi*, does sum it up pretty well."

"Simon, when Tom Joad conked the guard dead, you remember that?"

"I remember. His name was George, a camp guard. The bastard deserved it," Simon said. "A henchman, paid by money to bust up union organizers at any cost. He used an axe handle."

"It was good then? Conking him?" Peck asked.

"If you're using *conk* as a synonym for *kill*, my take is when living in desperate times, one needs desperate measures to survive."

"Can I sit with you two in court, Simon?"

"Of course," Simon said.

"What kind of book are you writing, Simon? Or is that a secret?"

"My editor wants me to expand a Cajun French character I created who seems to be garnering favor. He wants me to lead my character into a series of New Orleans mysteries. Not talking plot. I'm superstitious that way."

"I'm Cajun French."

The court doors opened and people filed in. The judge's chair was empty but assistants moved about getting things in place, preparing for the court to begin. Peck, Damas and Simon found seats by an aisle.

"Where do you live?"

"I live on Magazine Street," Damas said.

"Southampton," Simon said.

Peck stirred in his seat.

"Southampton? Is that anything like Hamptons?"

"It is the Hamptons. There are a number of towns in Southampton. Sag Harbor, Bridgehampton, Westhampton Beach, others."

"Aye-yi-yi. Are you staying at a hotel?" Peck asked.

"Nicole and I are at the Ponchartrain. On St. Charles."

"Ah *oui*."

"The wife's sleeping in. Late night with friends."

"Do you like jazz?"

"I do," Damas said.

"New Orleans jazz. Nicole and I love the sounds of this magical city," Simon said.

"How long in New Or-lee-anh?" Peck whispered.

"We're on a two o'clock flight, maybe next time."

Peck looked at Damas.

"Charlie's Blue Note tonight, frien'?"

"I'll come," Damas said.

"It's on Frenchman Street. I want you to meet my frien' Gabe. You'll like him. He can teach you a lot on Creole, dass for true."

Damas nodded as Peck eyed Lily Cup coming into the courtroom and stepping over to the clerk. She waved before sitting with a man.

As they waited for court to begin, Peck saw to it that Damas looked up Charlie's Blue Note and added it to his contacts. He added Peck's number as well. Peck started to turn off his phone. There was a text from Lily Cup on it.

"I need a ride home."

He texted back, "*oui*," and turned his phone off.

"Order in the Court, all rise. Section M of the Criminal District Court is now in session. Silence is commanded under penalty of fine or imprisonment. God save this state and this honorable court. Please be seated. Good morning, Judge."

The bailiff spoke with loud, officious resonance.

"The State of Louisiana calls Lebron Washington. The defendant will rise and be sworn," the bailiff said.

Lily Cup stood with her client.

Peck leaned into Simon to speak.

Simon held his index finger up over his closed lips, gesturing no talking while the judge was in the room.

Peck sat back and slumped as if he needed coffee and he regretted drinking so much brandy last night. His tracker eyes darted around the courtroom as if they were thoughts playing ping pong with a mission partially accomplished in the dead of a moonless night in the darkness of ghostly sheets of rain. *Is Simon Dermott an opportunity? Hamptons? Safest if I let Damas and Gabe talk tonight and I just listen. What does Lily Cup want with me today? Did a flash of lightning last night show my face to anyone? How long will I have to be with Lily Cup? When is my reconnaissance with Gabe goin' to start?*

At a point when the judge stood and went to her chamber for a conference, Peck confirmed that Damas would be at Charlie's. He left the courthouse to get his pickup, and started it as he crossed the street into the parking area. He pulled out and in front of the court house and waited for Lily Cup, his engine running. His phone rang. He didn't know the number calling.

"Hello?" Peck asked.

"Hi," a girl whispered.

"Who you are?" Peck asked.

"I just woke up. I saw your number."

"Do I know your voice, cher?"

"The number reminded me I feel like dancing."

Peck grinned, recognizing the voice.

"Aren't you supposed to be at work, frien'?"

"You have so many girls, bébé, you don't know who I am."

"You're Aurelie, cher. Pretty Aurelie, phone girl. How you are and why aren't you at work?"

"I don't go in until noon today. I worked last night. I was thinking of dancing tonight. Did you mean what you said—about teaching me jazz dancing?"

"Oh, I meant it, cher. Ever' word. I'll be with frien's there but I can dance with you, dass for true. Will you go with your girlfriend or be alone?"

"With my friend."

"Good," Peck said. "I see you at Charlie's tonight."

"Bye—" Aurelie started.

"Wait, bébé. Wait."

"What?"

"Can I ax you something?"

"Sure."

"I know this bad man, cher. He left his phone on a seat on the streetcar. Is it safe for Peck to maybe give it to the police or can somebody trace it?"

"Take the sim card out."

"Hanh?"

"Take the sim card out and throw the phone away. The phone can be traced. If he's a bad man, somebody he knows can trace that phone and know where it is. They probably traced it already. The sim card will have everything the police need."

Aurelie proceeded to give Peck instructions on removing the sim card. They said goodbye while Peck got out of the pickup and walked to a trash container. He slipped the sim card into his pocket and rubbed his prints from the phone before dropping it in and covering it in debris.

Lily Cup came out of the courthouse. She saw the pickup, paused in conversation with her client before walking down the long granite stairway and climbing into Peck's truck.

"Did you stay last night?" Lily Cup asked.

"Ah *oui*, cher. I put you to bed and slept in the other bedroom. I got up early and went to get some clothes and had coffee with Gabe before I come to court."

"I don't remember last night," Lily Cup said. "I've got to slow down."

"Wasn't it you telling me to slow down, cher?"

"No more rye."

"It's not what you drink, cher, it's how much."

"Good, I like my rye but too old to try to keep up."

Peck parked a block from Lily Cup's house.

"Why here, Peck?"

"Safer, cher."

They walked to the house, up the drive and in through the side kitchen door. Lily Cup pointed at the coffee thermos and excused herself while she ran upstairs. When she came down, she was in sweatpants and a Harvard Law T-shirt.

"Peck, I've got to get some sleep, will you be pissed?"

"Nah nah, cher. You up late last night reading and we ate too many tails and oysters. You sleep and I'll go and see Gabe or read me a book or something."

"Will you come back at three?"

"Do you have court tomorrow, cher?"

"No court until Monday."

"I meet an author in court today, cher. His research assistant was going to Charlie's tonight, so I can introduce him to Gabe. Can maybe you let Peck come tonight after Charlie's? That way you can rest all day, cher."

"I'll probably sleep until you get here. Let yourself in." She tossed him a key.

"Ah *oui*. This is good, cher. You be rested and we'll talk then."

"I'll make pancakes, so no beans at Charlie's, okay? I'll do grits and boudin."

"Yum," Peck said.

"In case Larry calls me, Peck, what did you do with the handbag you want him to lift the fingerprints from?"

"Who?"

"My detective friend, Larry."

Peck startled. He knew the bag was hidden upstairs in the second bedroom, but red tattoo man was dead now and he couldn't take any chances of being tied to his fingerprints —in any way. He had to throw Lily Cup off track. So he lied.

"Ah, cher—I take it to the shotgun."

"Why'd you take it over there?"

"For safekeeping. I'll get it when we need it."

"Are you sure you're going to come tonight?"

"I promise, cher. You sleep."

"Will you wake me up if I'm asleep?"

Peck leaned down, lifted her and hugged a goodbye.

"I promise to wake you, cher. Millie say to give you big hug. I see you later."

21.

AS PECK MADE HIS WAY to the pickup to drive home, Lily Cup's detective friend, Lieutenant Larry Gaines, entered the Orleans Parish coroner's lab. Coroner Chris O'Sullivan was standing over the table with a half-naked dead male body lying in underwear with an identification tag wired to his toe. The coroner was in surgical garb, with rubber gloves and a plastic face shield.

"Good morning, Lieutenant," O'Sullivan said.

"Chief didn't call me until this morning, Chris. Sorry if I've held you up."

"Not a problem, Lieutenant."

"Why is this body wearing underwear?"

"I was ordered to wait for you, since you didn't have the opportunity of inspecting it at the scene. Now that you're here I have to wait for forensics to come and cut them off for lab testing. Forensics is on their way."

"Fill me in with what you know, Chris—time of death, place, what do we know?"

"Don't you want *cause of death*, Lieutenant?"

"I already know cause of death, that's why the chief called me in on it. He said the MO fits the Porsche homicide I'm on— the Storyville murder and blow to the head."

"Well, it almost fits it, Lieutenant. I'm not sure yet."

"What do you mean?"

"My first thought was a man in his underwear came outside in the rain, he slipped and fell somehow, hitting his head."

"That makes sense," Lieutenant Gaines said.

"Lieutenant, if I was a betting man, I'd bet this was a copycat murder."

"Oh?"

"I can't prove it, but look at the mark on the skull."

"Looks like one blow."

"Now look at this picture of the Porsche corpse. Look at the mark on his skull."

"Looks identical," Lieutenant Gaines said.

"Identical!" O'Sullivan said.

"What do you make of it, Chris— coincidence?"

"Same killer, maybe. Same weapon maybe."

"But you said *almost*. What did you mean by that?"

"If it's homicide it's a different MO, Lieutenant."

"Something's not making sense, Chris. Start at the top. What am I missing? What are you thinking?"

"Your Porsche victim was sitting in his car, safely buckled in—with his skull crushed. His car was in reverse at the time, supposedly while backing out of an alley—one clean blow, no windows broken, no prints, and the car backed into a utility box and stalled out. All of this is in the forensic report. His suit was Armani. It had to be a five thousand dollar suit."

"And underwear guy here? Wasn't in a car. Is that your point?"

"That's just it, Lieutenant. Found this one stretched out on his back on the steps outside his own front door. In the pouring rain. In his underwear. No door kicked in, no Armani suit, no fancy car leaving a scene. The door was wide open and EMS reported nobody home."

"How did EMS get involved?"

"A man was walking his dog in the rain. His dog saw the body lying there and yelped. The man called 911."

"And the EMS saw the dead body and called the PD. They called you?" Lieutenant Gaines asked.

"Pretty much like that."

"Was there any evidence the home was empty when it happened or any signs it emptied out after the homicide, if it was a homicide?"

"None. While I was determining time of death, an officer on the scene told me there was a hundred and seventy thousand in cash and some handwritten debit card receipts on the kitchen island, along with a money-counting machine. That's not my area, Lieutenant, but my guess is if someone was in the house and ran, the money would have taken off with them."

A man and a woman from forensics walked into the lab.

"Morning, folks. Is that the body?"

"It is," O'Sullivan said.

Standing on either side of the table, the forensics team scissor-snipped the body's T-shirt and briefs. They reached under the lower back of the body and lifted it enough to pull the briefs and t-shirt off. With tweezers they removed the diamond stud earrings. They bagged everything and left the room.

"Good day, gentlemen," the forensic lady said.

Larry leaned down to examine the dollar sign tattoo.

"Lieutenant," O'Sullivan said. "Something caught my eye when they lifted him. Can you help me turn him over?"

As the body was rolled onto its side and then plopped face down on the table, Coroner O'Sullivan pointed at a series of tattoos on the corpse's buttocks.

"Look at these," O'Sullivan said.

"What in the hell is all that?" Larry asked.

"These tattoos look like barcodes, Lieutenant."

"Barcodes? You mean barcodes like at a grocery? Soup or butter barcodes?"

"They're upside down, two inches apart. Lieutenant, my guess is these barcode tattoos may be some sort of secret record of drug dealers."

"I don't buy it, Chris. As volatile and as momentary as a drug pusher's connections are, I don't see permanently branding somebody on your ass who might be dead on a whim."

"Maybe he's a trafficker, Lieutenant."

"That makes more sense. Trafficking is a whole new world today in inner cities. It's organizing fast, and it's doing big dollars. The red dollar sign tattoo could be a pimp sign," Lieutenant Gaines said. "I've seen it before."

"These bar codes could be his girls or their prices," O'Sullivan said.

"Or boys," Lieutenant Gaines said.

"Or boys," O'Sullivan said.

"So, a john orders one of his sex slaves by phone, he goes into a men's room stall, drops his pants. He takes a credit card number, scans the right barcode on his ass and runs the charge before he drops the girl or boy at the john's hotel. No proof of anything on him. Pulls his pants up and washes his hands."

"You're good, Lieutenant. You're very good."

"If he's a sex trafficker, those girls and boys are his permanent inventory and won't be going anywhere unless it's feet first in body bags," Lieutenant Gaines said. "I'm going to go check out the scene. I have a search warrant. See if you can get those bar codes read. If you do, let's keep it between us for a while. I'll be back. Call me if you need me."

As Lieutenant Gaines left the morgue, Gabe and Peck stepped off a streetcar and walked to Canal Street.

"Gabe you work the concierges on this side of Canal Street and I'll do the other side."

"My reconnaissance was dead on, son, about who I think are Cajun or Cajun French, but when you go in the hotel to get a concierge's attention, make sure for yourself."

"Ah *Oui*."

Peck took Gabe's hand and with a marker he wrote a phone number on the fleshy pink of his palm.

"Gabe, if we feel right with them, we give them this phone number, and have them text it to say where paid sex is happening. Make sure you tell them to text only, never call it or leave messages, and don't forget to tell them to delete their text right after they send it."

"Got it."

"We'll switch sides of Canal Street after we get to the end of block three. After Canal you go in the Quarter, Gabe, I'm going to Jackson Square for something."

"And you won't tell me whose number this is, son?"

"Captain, you don't need to know—better you don't know. Wash it off your hand when we're done."

They turned from each other and began the mission. In a matter of three hours, they had befriended nineteen hotel concierges, some black, some Cajun French. Sixteen accepted the phone number. Three didn't accept it while promising secrecy. They approved, but were afraid of being found out and targeted by the underworld.

Peck told Gabe he'd be home later to drive him to Charlie's. He turned and walked to Jackson Square to see if the St. Louis Basilica was open.

22.

IN THE BASILICA Peck pushed folded bills into the slot and lighted three candles. The majestic church temple was empty and illuminated by sunlight beaming through colorful holy scenes on painted glass. He genuflected at the center aisle and walked to the altar in front. He knelt at the Communion rail and blessed himself. Elbows on the rail, he clasped his hands and looked up at the hanging cross of Jesus, the crucifixion and whispered.

"God, you know what I done."

He paused in thought.

"I can't lie to you. I done it, dass for true. What I gonna' try to do is to ax you to please understand that I didn't conk those men for hate. God, I didn't conk them because I think it was right because my father and that gator man got killed dead. I didn't learn it was right from them killings, God. I learned it from you I think, and I learned it from my mamma. I may be wrong, God, but I think I learned that children—how you say—in the eyes of God are the world. I conk them men to help save that little girl is all, a child of God."

Peck closed his eyes. A tear slid down his cheek. He rested his face in his hands, thinking. A police siren outside broke his concentration. He looked up at the cross.

"God, I did something else today, but I don't know what will happen from that, and dass for true. I hope you're not mad at Peck, God, and you will give me a chance to come back after I think about it good and tell you how sorry I am. I'll do the confession with Father McBride, I promise, God."

He blessed himself, stood and walked the aisle to the front doors and left the church. Standing in Jackson Square, Peck dialed his friend Elizabeth in Baton Rouge. He had met Elizabeth in Anse La Butte on a 103-degree day when he was seventeen and she was twenty-two. He had just thrown his trotline into a bayou near where she lived and was in a convenience store buying bottled water when they met and became friends.

Illiterate at the time, he would walk the eleven miles from the hospice where he mowed lawns in Carencro to Breaux Bridge to be with her on lonely nights. If she was alone, her code was a lighted candle on the mantle. She wasn't married, but she had a boyfriend who worked offshore on oil rigs, and he'd be gone six weeks at a time. Peck and Elizabeth became best friends and they would sit for hours in a bathtub together, as if it was their treehouse, he washing her back with a soft, soapy sponge and her clipping his toenails while they talked of his fishing catches and of her day at the Creole chicken restaurant, and of her dreams of a cooking academy and of crepes with marmalade and jams, and her dream of someday cooking in Paris.

"*Est-ce que c'est toi, Peck?*" ("Is this you, Peck?")

"*Bonjour cher, comment vas-tu?*" ("Hello cher, how you are?") "*Parlez anglais, cher.*" ("Speak English, cher.")

"I'm graduating in a month, Peck. Can you and Millie come to my graduation from the cooking school?"

"Ah *oui*, cher. We be there. How's rig man?"

"We broke up, Peck. It's all good. We're friends, but it's over. He moved out."

"Do you still work at the bistro, cher?"

"Yes, but I'm moving to Paris after I graduate. I want to be a chef in Paris."

"Ah *oui*, cher, you always dreamed of Paris. I dream of my crawfish farm with my Millie someday, and I dream of you in Paris cooking for important people."

"How is Millie, Peck?"

"Millie is so good, cher."

"I'll mail you both an invitation."

"Cher, do you still see the Tarot lady? The reader?"

"Audrey? I do, why?"

"I need to see Audrey, cher. Can I maybe come up tomorrow, and you ax if I can see her?"

"Yes. I'm off tomorrow so I can go with you if you'd like."

"Nah nah, cher. I need to go see Audrey with a frien'. Peck has some things on my mind … some things in my head I need to ax her about. Can I bring a frien' with me?"

"Of course. Do you know what time you'll get here?"

"I go to Charlie's tonight, then I got to go to Lily Cup's. If I wake up early how early tomorrow can I come, cher?"

"You know the gate code, Peck. Come anytime you get finished with Audrey. Just ring the bell."

"I see you tomorrow cher."

Peck walked to St. Charles and caught a streetcar home to the shotgun.

23.

IN STORYVILLE, Lieutenant Larry Gaines's phone rings. He picks up.

"I'm busy, make it fast," he barks.

"Chris here, Lieutenant."

"What'cha got?"

"I found bruising, Lieutenant."

"I saw his forehead, Chris."

"More than that, Lieutenant. I came back from lunch and I found post-mortem bruising on his scalp, above the hairline."

"And that wasn't there before?"

"It just appeared. Happens sometimes, especially if someone was drowned."

"Was he drowned, Chris?"

"No, but his nasal cavity and throat were filled with rain water."

"Maybe he was pulled down by the hair?" Larry asked.

"That's what I'm thinking Lieutenant."

"So, maybe we are talking homicide," Larry said.

"It's looking like that, Lieutenant."

"Any chance of finding the attacker's DNA from the hair, Chris?"

"There was, but that's probably bad news, Lieutenant. I'll know more this afternoon."

"What bad news?"

"When the body was brought in, my assistant was on duty, and he received a call from the police chief telling him to hold the body untouched, and that you would be by in the morning to examine it, if he could find you."

"Well, he found me an hour before I came in. I was in Covington with my phone off. So, what's the bad news?"

"The deceased was in a plastic body bag all night and he was wet. Moist plastic provides a growth environment for bacteria ..."

"And?"

"And that bacterium destroys DNA evidence."

"Do what you can, Chris. Meantime, guess what I found?"

"You know if it's drug or trafficker," Chris said. "Which?"

"Big-time sex trafficker. I found a box of USB Flash Drives. Pictures of girls. We'll see what they have on them."

"How big, Lieutenant?"

"If this hundred and seventy thousand bucks was a one-week pull, it might mean twenty-four sex slaves."

"This could be a find for New Orleans, Lieutenant."

"Could be. We'll see what's on these USB drives. We'll see if there are any clues on them as to where the slaves are being held. Somebody has got to have made a mistake somewhere. I'm locking the house down. Forensics is coming."

"Good idea. I'll let you know if I find anything else with this body or the barcodes."

24.

PECK AND GABE STEPPED UP into Charlie's Blue Note. Simon Dermott's research assistant, Damas, was standing by the bar with a beer in his hand, listening to jazz, waiting. He offered his hand and a smile. Peck introduced him to Gabe.

"Pleasure to meet a brother," Gabe said. "Always a pleasure to see a brother looking dapper, bow tie, nice cut in your suit."

"Good of you to have me tonight, Captain."

"That captain talk is past tense, son. I retired before you were born. Let's use Gabe."

Their table was open, and after Gabe's cordial salutations to Charlie and some other friends he recognized, Gabe and Damas made their way while Peck went to the backroom order window for bowls of red beans and rice. He noticed that André was not at the bar.

"You a jazz aficionado son? The blues? What's your pleasure, my brother?" Gabe asked.

"I pretty much like music, Gabe," Damas said. "Momma made me take three years of piano lessons."

"A good momma, indeed, son. Mine made me read a chapter and tell her about it before I could go outside and play. My daddy was a piano tuner. He taught me jazz."

"My momma made me play for her friends when they came to the house," Damas said. "I had to put on a show for them of at least two pieces. Then I had to stand up and take a bow."

Gabe laughed. "And to what do we owe this pleasure?" he asked.

"My boss and I met Peck in court today, and he was nice enough to invite me here to meet you and to listen to some jazz, of course. That's pretty much it. He said I would find your Creole background interesting, especially in my line of work."

"And that is?" Gabe asked.

"Well, I work at a bookstore for my regular income, but I'm a part-time research assistant for a writer. A book writer. He hired me to do groundwork in Louisiana."

Peck came to the table carrying a tray with bowls of red beans and rice, the utensils, napkins, a tumbler of Chivas and a long neck beer. He sat.

"Would I know the writer?" Gabe asked.

"Simon Dermott. He has some novels out. He's got me studying southern Louisiana, the Acadian culture. He's thinking of writing a mystery. I'm doing his legwork."

"The name Dermott has an Irish cut to it, son. Is this Simon Dermott from here?"

"He lives in the Hamptons. I'm not sure where he came from originally."

"If it's the Hamptons I've read about, that's some high cotton, my brother. You're in good company."

"It's the same Hamptons. He writes his books there."

"How lucky are you, brother, to get to work with a man like that?"

"I know. He comes here a few times a year for book signings and to meet with me. It's great fun. I learn a lot and I get to earn some extra money."

"It sounds like a life-fulfilling notch on your belt of experiences, my brother. Imagine getting to research for an author who's looking for ideas. How was Simon Dermott lucky enough to happen upon you, a brother from the Big Easy?"

"He was staying at the Ponchartrain Hotel, in—"

"I know the Ponchartrain, son. Tennessee Williams lived there. He wrote *Streetcar Named Desire* there. Truman Capote would visit him. Frank Sinatra and friends would meet them for drinks at the bar. I've been to Silver Whistle on more than one occasion. How did you happen into each other there?"

"I was working a weekend job as elevator host from the lobby to the Hot Tin, the roof garden bar. Extra money. That's how we met."

"So, you hosted an author up the elevator."

"Actually, my job was to count how many got on the elevator and how many got off so the Hot Tin didn't get more people than fire code allowed. It wasn't as glamorous a job as it sounds, but it paid, and I have two sons, and there were occasional tips."

"Isn't it amazing what opportunities happen to us if we just keep productive and busy, regardless of what we're doing? Your sons are lucky boys to have such a good father."

"Why thank you, Gabe."

"I mean it, my brother."

"Simon wanted to see what the Hot Tin was all about and to consider it for a new book launch party."

"Did you know who he was when he walked up?"

"No, but that's how we met, he was waiting in line for my elevator."

"Interesting."

"I admired his bowtie. He took it off and handed it to me. Actually, it's this one I'm wearing."

"My brother."

"I asked the front desk for his email so I could thank him properly and the next thing I knew, I was doing research and spending three hours with New Orleans own, the famous Leah Chase in her kitchen at the Dooky Chase restaurant."

"Leah Chase is New Orleans, son. Simon Dermott is a smart man."

"Ms. Chase invited me into her kitchen. I got to interview her on the history of New Orleans through her eyes. Simon had written questions for me to ask her and she answered every one of them with a smile."

"You've been blessed, my brother. What a lady. What a story. Peck thank you for bringing this young man."

The band took a break and as the saxophone player walked by, long dark bronze fingers patted Gabe's shoulder a gentle hello. Gabe grabbed the hand on his shoulder and stood.

"Brother, will you take our picture?"

"My pleasure," the sax player said. "Whose phone?"

"I don't own a phone. Peck, can he use yours?"

Peck handed his phone over, and they stood by Gabe, hamming poses. Gabe had them take one with each of them holding their drinks up in a toast, Gabe's hand gripped his tumbler over Damas's shoulder. The saxophone player handed the phone back to Peck with a smile and walked away. Sitting down, Peck texted the pictures to Millie with some heart emoticons and one he thought the best to Damas. Millie texted back: *I have an idea for my paper. I love you, give Gabe a big hug.*

Peck received another text.

"Nous sommes là, Peck. Es tu là?" ("We're here, Peck. Are you here?")

Peck stood and looked around. In another corner were two girls at a small table. One was his telephone friend, Aurelie.

"Gabe, Damas, I have a friend come in. I promised to dance with her. Then I'm meeting Lily Cup. Do you mind if I leave? She's such a purdy girl?" He shook Damas's hand, then Gabe's.

"Gabe, tomorrow I'm goin' to Baton Rouge."

"You're leaving me in good company, son. We'll be fine. Sasha will be here later and she'll see me home."

"Thanks for inviting me to meet Gabe, Peck. Will I see you in court?" Damas asked.

"Dass for true, frien', this week or next week sure."

They shook hands again and Peck turned and walked to Aurelie's table.

"What kind of research are you doing, son?" Gabe asked. "How can an old black Creole help a brother?"

"Simon got an email from the mayor," Damas said.

"The New Orleans mayor?"

"Yes sir, the mayor was asking if a book could bring awareness to a growing sex trafficking problem. It's taking over cities."

Gabe bolted, sat up straight.

"Damas, does Peck know what you're researching?"

"I don't recall telling him—didn't have time. We only met the few minutes we were together in the court."

"What are you looking for in the court, my brother? Sex trafficking cases?"

"Actually, I'm making a dictionary of the terms used in New Orleans courtrooms—the vernacular, the give and take. I'm doing this so Simon can write believable dialogue, as he would say, with authentic local color."

"Interesting, son. What does this have to do with sex trafficking?"

"Nothing, Gabe. Trafficking is his part of it."

"You've lost me, son."

Damas lifted his satchel and pulled out a folder.

"The mayor contacted Simon for two reasons, Gabe. Writing was one. He's a talented storyteller. But the mayor told him his career in marketing before he became a writer might help him come up with a way to build awareness for the problem. Awareness nobody seems to be able to do."

Damas pulled a sheet out and glanced at excerpts.

"They want the public to be aware of trafficking in America, Gabe. Americans relate trafficking to border issues, not local problems that affect their lives."

"Is that what your notes say, son?"

"Yes, this is an email from Simon telling why most adults find no problem or sex trafficking threat with stripper bars, lap dances, that sort of thing. The average American thinks of them as harmless fun."

"I can see that, brother. A lap dance seems harmless enough. Honest women struggling to try to put food on the table. A boy's night out."

Damas lifted another page. "Listen to this, Gabe:

'Sex traffickers have a sinister market that is seeded by publicly-accepted sex entertainment. Pornography for one, another is a 'front' of women who appear publicly to choose to strip on their own accord. They do and they are free to come and go and not ever go under public scrutiny to be considered sex slaves, as the public doesn't see them as sex slaves. People will not hold a patron of a strip club accountable for contributing to sex slavery as they just see it as a stretch. It's entertainment, like porn is. Prostitution is

the oldest profession, and it's thought of in voluntary terms. A business transaction.'"

"That sounds like it pretty much gets titty bars and strippers off the hook, doesn't it, son?"

"It does until you read this, Gabe:

'Traffickers are the ultimate in marketing. They are masters with numbers. Traffickers know 15% of the public is willing to perform criminal acts. If a strip club can open up and run a publicly-accepted strip club with, let's say, 60 strippers— nine of the girls there will be willing and open to taking married men into private VIP rooms for sex, paid for with orders of $5,000—$10,000 bottles of champagne. Some girls will use date rape drugs to steal expensive watches and charge their credit cards with tens of thousands of dollars— charging their victim's cards to limits they know married men could never discuss with their wives.'"

"What you're saying, son, is some stripper bars put up false fronts of a club we think is just for kicks, naughty looks and lap dances, but they're counting on mathematical numbers in bad behavior—what it takes to fleece millions out of married men every week by just a handful of those strippers?"

"Yes, Gabe. Simon said numbers don't lie. They play the numbers. Most of the girls don't think of it that way, but they're connecting lap dance titillation of a pay-for-innocent sex-fun front with trafficking."

"So, if a titty bar has a back room, look out?"

"Pretty much, Gabe. The girls in front just trying to earn a living don't know they are just that—a front for big money back rooms."

"Son, I'm proud to make your acquaintance. You taught this old bird something new. Now let's enjoy our beans and rice."

As Gabe and Damas spooned into their bowls, Peck finished dancing with his phone friend, Aurelie. He left Charlie's and was soon stepping into Lily Cup's kitchen, finding her heating an iron skillet for the bacon and boudin she had waiting on a cutting board.

"How you are, cher?"

"Thermos is full, Peck, and that's all we drink tonight. Have a seat. I'll make pancakes."

She sashayed her hips, butting the refrigerator door closed, and handed Peck a small bowl of left-over crawfish to get him started.

25.

PECK'S EVENING WITH LILY CUP was about food and the good memories they shared, and how she got the zest of lemon in her pancakes.

Lily Cup spoke of the fifteen-year-old in court who held up a 7-Eleven with his brother's 45-caliber handgun for a cigarette lighter. Peck spoke of needing spackling for Mamma's houseboat. Lily Cup, rested and confident that Peck had slowed down, helped him relax.

Peck mentioned his going to Baton Rouge in the morning to see Audrey, the Tarot card reader. It was midnight when Lily Cup tucked Peck in her guest bed and sat on the bed cross-legged in panties and Harvard Law T-shirt talking about what she might wear to the N'Orleans spring cotillion and would Millie let Peck escort her again.

Peck closed his eyes and fell asleep midsentence. Lily Cup leaned over and switched his bedside lamp off. She went to her room, stripped her T-shirt and panties off, tossed them in the general direction of a clothes hamper and crawled into her own bed.

In time Peck's snoring stirred her. She went quietly into his room, lifted his blanket and in a moon beam, admired his body and the stout William resting on his inner thigh. She crawled in, hoping her chill wouldn't awaken him and snuggled back into his curves and fell asleep in the warmth of the memories of their friendship.

When Lily Cup awakened, she found herself nestled with a pillow between her knees and alone with the morning sun warming a bedside table. Peck was gone. She rolled on her back and smiled at the ceiling. She imagined him on the road, on his way to Baton Rouge. She envisioned Elizabeth's crepes and her marmalade and jams and perhaps Audrey's Tarot cards bringing a calming focus to Peck, and making sense of the world around him.

As Lily Cup wrestled with whether soaking in a tub bath or taking a shower would be her start to the day, Peck, who she thought was on route to Baton Rouge, was stepping onto a Bourbon Street sidewalk. He was looking for Pedicab B25. Not to be an obvious standout, he walked the sidewalk at a careful distance, looking at reflections off antique store and coffee shop windows until he saw it, the pedicab he was looking for. He pulled a twenty from his pocket, turned and visually confirmed it was Lauren. He walked over and held out the twenty. Lauren stood, as if readying to start pedaling and took the money from him.

"Jes' a few blocks, that be good, cher?"

"Hop in," Lauren said, like she didn't know him.

She stood, pushed her stomach against the handle bars and walked the pedicab forward about ten feet from the others. She stepped up on the pedals and gradually brought it up to speed, looking both ways and watching traffic for safety. She had pedaled two city blocks before they spoke.

"How you are, bébé?"

"Not so good."

"Oh? What's wrong?"

"My roommate."

"Nah-nah, bébé. She's quitting, right?"

"Yup. Told me she might move to Florida."

"That's not good. Can you find a partner maybe?"

"I'm asking around. If she takes off, paying for this thing alone will dig into my savings."

"You'll find somebody, bébé."

"You didn't come for a ride, did you?"

"Nah nah, dass for true."

"Coffee?"

"Sure."

Lauren pedaled to a bike stand and chained the pedicab. They walked to a beignet shop, sat outside.

"What's up?" Lauren asked.

"I need to go to Baton Rouge, bébé."

"Why Baton Rouge?"

"I know a reader there."

"Tarot?"

"Ah *oui*."

"When?"

"Like now. I have a frien' I stay with in Baton Rouge, Elizabeth. You'd like her. Want to come with me, bébé?"

"How do I know you're not one of those bastards?"

"Aw bébé. Don't you know Peck by now? I'm on the good side. We can talk there, not worry who's seein' us."

"You were going to get fingerprints. Where are the prints, and where's my bag?"

"My lawyer frien'. She gettin' a detective to get the prints looked at bébé, dass for true. I'm thinkin' go now and come back tomorrow—if you like Tarot."

"I like readers," Lauren said.

"Dass good, cher."

"What do cards have to do with Baton Rouge?"

"Audrey is in Baton Rouge, cher—a good Tarot reader. We'll stay with Elizabeth. You'll like her crepes and jam and her coddled eggs with white pepper. So good."

"There's some nursing schools in Baton Rouge. Can I check them out?"

"Ah *oui*, bébé. Lots of time. Ever'thing close by in Baton Rouge."

"Hold on," Lauren said.

She lifted her phone and texted her roommate, asked if she might come to Bourbon Street and spell her for that day and the next. Her roommate asked why. Lauren texted a smile emoticon and made up a story about having a chance to hook up with a dude and wanted a couple of days off. Her roommate (and pedicab partner) said yes. Lauren texted where the pedicab was parked and that she'd be leaving right away.

"I need to stop for clothes," Lauren said.

"Nah, nah, cher."

"Not walking in nursing schools looking like this."

"My lawyer boss jes' paid me for cleaning her offices all month. How much an outfit cost, bébé?"

"Twenty, maybe."

Peck handed her a twenty.

"We'll stop someplace. You'll like Elizabeth."

"Okay."

Peck leaned in to whisper. "Walk to Burgundy Street, keep walking down three blocks, bébé. I'm going the other way and get my pickup. When you see me coming, jes' get in like you know me."

Peck stood and walked away, a coffee in his hand.

As Peck and Lauren drove into Baton Rouge, Lily Cup was at home, still in her tub. Her phone rested on the small table next to her hot bubble bath. It rang. She looked at the screen, and saw that it was Lieutenant Detective Larry Gaines. She wiped suds from her hand and touched it.

"Hi Larry, what's up?"

"Still combing through evidence on two murders. I just remembered you needed to trace prints."

"Two murders? You're a busy dude."

"Coroner thinks they're connected, that's why I'm on them. I'm still looking for the little details as always. How about your prints? I have a window open."

"I don't know where that stands, Larry. It could have been a false alarm. I'll have to let you know."

"Call me if you need them."

"Thanks, Larry."

"Why the echo, Lily Cup? Where are you?"

"In my bathtub. All wrinkly and cozy warm."

"Ain't nothin' finer than a beautiful criminal attorney naked in a bubble bath. Oh my."

"Why Larry—ha! And you a happily married man."

"My lady is having second thoughts. Says she needs more of a nine-to-five guy."

"What world does she live in?"

"Not mine. She's living with her mamma, thinking it over."

"I do love brown sugar," Lily Cup mused.

"I'll keep that in mind, naked lady," Larry said with a smirk as he hung up.

26.

PECK AND LAUREN APPROACHED Audrey's door for their reading, speaking of last-minute briefings.

Hearing them, Audrey pulled the door open. "Come in," she said, as she hung a *Do Not Disturb* sign on the front doorknob.

Her eyes had a welcoming smile. Her red hair was tied back into a ponytail. She was wearing a black sweatshirt and jeans. She was freckle-faced, and probably in her forties.

The first room was dark with window shades drawn and three candles on the same dish in the middle of the table. Light from their wicks flickered shadows on images on the walls and shelves, like waves washing ashore. There were images of a statue of the Virgin Mary, and rosary beads hung from bookshelves.

Audrey took Peck and Lauren by the hands.

Oh my," she said.

"What?" Peck asked.

"Touching your hands. They're moist, warm."

There was no response.

"Did you bring decks?" Audrey asked.

"Nah nah," Peck said, "Can we buy some?"

"Of course. Let's go into the next room."

The second room was dark, but with a red glow to it, no book shelves, no statues or decorations on the walls. It had one round, oak table in the center with three chairs around it. A velvet cloth covered the table. A lamp wire hung above the center of the table with a glowing red bulb. A fourth chair sat next to a wall.

Lauren and Peck each took a seat around the table. Before sitting, Audrey handed each of them their decks.

"A Tarot card reading is a mystical experience that can help you better understand your unique journey through the spiritual, emotional, and physical world. It gives you a glimpse within, offering you a mirror into your own soul. I always start by listening to why you think you've come for a reading. Today we may do it a little differently. Peck, I've had the honor of knowing your soul from past visits and readings. I know that you are not of a kind to travel all this way unless there wasn't something important to discuss. And Lauren, we've never met, but you have traveled with Peck such a distance. I feel we need to go deeper on our introduction of topics. Can either or both of you share what you are searching to learn?"

"Miss Audrey, a nine-year-old was sold to a bad man for sex," Peck said. "Now she's twelve and we've got to save her. I've already done some bad things trying, dass for true, but I need—how you say—guidance."

"Are you saying this man paid to have sex with a nine-year-old?" Audrey asked.

"Nah, nah, this man bought her and now he owns her like a slave," Peck said.

Peck sat back and Lauren leaned in.

"The girl is thirteen, Ms. Audrey. I have a pedicab, and one night one of her johns didn't want her because she was starting her period, and I tried to help her run away, but her pimp caught us and beat her, threatened me with a gun and took her away," Lauren said. "I promised Peck I would help find her."

"Oh, my Lord. I'm not certain what reading can do … Does this girl have a name?"

"The only name I know is Tiffany. Her pimp makes her use Tiffany. I don't know her real name," Lauren said.

"We can try. For the sake of Tiffany, please shuffle your cards."

Peck and Lauren shuffled. Lauren hand to hand, Peck fanning his cards and mixing them on the table and then picking them up. Audrey took Lauren's deck and fanned the cards out, face down.

"Lauren, pass your hand over your cards and select two cards. Select the two cards you feel are speaking to you."

Lauren flattened her right hand and lowered it inches above her fanned-out deck. She passed them over and back, left to right and back over again. She pointed at a card, pushed it out and then to another and pushed it out.

"I feel something with these," Lauren said.

Audrey took Peck's deck and fanned them face down on the table.

"Peck, pass your hand over your cards and select the two cards you feel speaking to you."

With cold, gray eyes, Peck flicked a finger out like a Cobra's tongue and pointed it to a card and pushed it from the fanned deck to Audrey. He repeated the point and pushed another.

"Here," Peck said.

Audrey closed her eyes and lowered her head for several minutes. She raised her head.

"I have a bad feeling," Audrey said. "I feel danger."

She clasped her hands as if in prayer.

"I must ask if either of you know of any reason why I should be feeling suffering or maybe death?"

"Yes," Peck whispered.

"Are you certain you want to proceed? Something's going on. I feel we should proceed with caution."

"I'm okay," Lauren said.

"I'm ready," Peck said. "Dass for true."

Audrey turned their cards. She looked and gasped. She clasped her hands and held them to her lips.

"Peck, you've selected a Moon card, which was your sign, we know from before, but you also selected this card— *The 10 of Swords*. It's a dangerous card, showing a man lying on the ground with ten swords stabbed in his back. You can see his red cape pulled back and the swords standing like they're crosses in a darkened sky."

She paused.

"Peck, you are involved with death or dangerously close to dead or death? Something with life passing."

"Ah *oui*," Peck muttered.

"Do you feel it, Peck?"

"Ah *oui*."

"Hold hands as we pray for your soul. You are carrying a heavy burden, and you need prayer at this time. Bow your head, repeat after me— *Lord have mercy on Peck.*

Do not look upon Peck's sins but take away all his guilt. Create in Peck a clean heart and renew within him an upright spirit. Amen."

Peck repeated the prayer. Audrey released his hand, paused and reflected. Then she turned to Lauren.

"Lauren, you selected the Sun card, which is positive, so you have a great deal of hope, but this one is *The Tower* card. The Tower card is a dangerous card. Have you been threatened?"

"Yes."

"You were spared for a reason?"

"He let me go," Lauren said. "But he took Tiffany, and he took all my money."

"Your card depicts a tall tower and two people falling headfirst from the tower and screaming. Your card shows trauma, fear, helplessness."

"Yes."

"Lauren, hold my hand. You've been traumatized, but your fears are not for yourself."

"For Tiffany."

"Lauren, pray for the soul you fear for?"

"Yes, please."

"Bow your head and repeat after me—*Grant, O Lord, thy protection for Tiffany and in protection, strength, understanding. And in understanding for Tiffany, knowledge. And in knowledge for Tiffany, the knowledge of justice."*

"That was perfect," Lauren said. "Thank you."

"Peck, were the cards you turned and my reading true, for this moment in time in your life?"

"It is, dass for true, Audrey."

"Lauren, are the cards you've turned true for this moment in time in your life?"

"Yes, they are."

"Lauren you've been traumatized. Do you need guidance? I can suggest a good therapist."

"Miss Audrey, I made a promise I would help until we find her. I'll keep my promise. When we're done, I'll go back and finish nursing school. I only have one more year."

"Peck, Lauren, I'm treading uncomfortable paths. I suggest we turn cards for yes or no answers to questions. This is a way of seeing the star paths."

"Ah *oui*," Peck said.

"I'd like that," Lauren said.

Audrey took both decks, shuffled them together and fanned them out in one large circle.

"Ask a question, Lauren," Audrey said.

"Is Tiffany okay?"

"Both of you select a card and pull it from the deck. Leave it on the table."

They picked cards, slid them to Audrey, who turned one at a time.

"Lauren, you selected *The Empress* card. This is a negative card. *The Empress* card sees issues and problems for Tiffany needing to be addressed before it is too late."

Audrey turned Peck's card.

"Peck, you selected *The Devil* card. A destroyer of families. Tiffany is in danger, and waiting for her next life."

Lauren broke into tears.

"Peck, you have a question?"

"Will we save Tiffany?"

"Lauren and Peck, pick a card."

Each selected and slid a card over to Audrey, who turned Peck's card first.

"Peck you selected *The Hanged Man* card. It suggests an end to a tyrant. A new beginning. It's a negative card, but there could be hope in it. It could destroy the foe."

Audrey turned Lauren's card.

"Lauren, you selected, *Knight of Pentacles*, directly linked to money, the financial realm. This is a positive card. The combinations of your cards send messages to me that Tiffany is in danger. She was being used for money by evil people and if you don't save her from this life soon, she could be sacrificed."

Peck tightened his fists and held them to his lips. Lauren sobbed. They stood, stepped out of the room and walked to the door. Peck held a credit card out for payment. Audrey gently pushed his hand away.

"There is no time to waste. Go save this girl."

"God bless you," Lauren said.

Peck gave Audrey a hug goodbye.

"Peck, don't be afraid of asking the police for help. Please keep me informed."

"I be back when it's over, Audrey, dass for true. Thank you. Thank you so much."

Peck and Lauren headed to Elizabeth's.

27.

ELIZABETH CRACKED THE DOOR OPEN, saw it was Peck and pulled it open wide. Arms as wide as her smile. Two white labels sticking from her black T-shirt apparently hurriedly pulled on inside out, to answer the door. She was wearing cooking school chef pants with a cotton string waist tie. Peck walked into arms that wrapped around him like layers of a fine French pastry.

"Tu me manques tellement, mon ami. M'avez-vous complètement oublié?" Elizabeth whispered. ("I miss you so much, my friend. Have you forgotten me completely?")

"Vous oublier serait comme oublier la lune," Peck said. ("Forgetting you would be like forgetting the moon.")

Elizabeth held his cheeks in her hands and kissed his mouth generously, warmly, passionately wet.

"Come to Paris with me?" she asked.

Elizabeth smiled, knowing it could only be a dream. She loved Peck enough to know he needed his trot lines and crawfish and his Millie, and all she needed at the moment was to be wearing her hard-earned *toque blanche* (chef's hat) at some fancy Paris bistro on the Left Bank with Saturday matinee visits to La Louvre and walks along the Champs-Elysees.

"Cher, I brought somebody. Okay if she stays?"

"She?"

"It's important, I can explain it good."

"Where is she?"

"In my pickup."

"Bring her up. I have to run to school for a graduation picture, but it'll only be an hour."

"Ah, so good, cher. Thanks."

"I have to get dressed. Get your friend."

Peck and Lauren came in the apartment as Elizabeth walked down the hall toward the kitchen. She was bare-breasted and in her scrubs, carrying a hanger with a starched and pressed white cooking school uniform coat with name tag attached.

"Elizabeth, this is Lauren. She's goin' to be a nurse, a good person from Oklahoma, before New Or-lee-anh. We all be friens'."

The girls exchanged hellos. Elizabeth assured Lauren that Peck was for real as she handed a hanger to Peck to hold while she reached for something in an upper cabinet.

"Are those medical scrubs?" Lauren asked.

"Ah *oui*, they have cooking pants but these are more comfortable. As long as my chef jacket is spotless, starched and pressed and my name tag is straight, they're good with scrubs."

"They breathe," Lauren said.

Elizabeth looked at the clock.

"Gotta' run," Elizabeth said. "You'll tell me about your visit with Audrey after I get back, and tonight we'll go to Bistro?"

"Ah *oui*," Peck said.

Elizabeth buttoned her coat and stepped out of the house and Peck gave Lauren a tour.

"This is the bedroom. If you're okay with sharing, you sleep with us tonight, bébé, or the couch in the living room is good."

"The couch is fine," Lauren said.

He pushed open the bathroom door and turned the light on.

"This the *salle de Bains* (bathroom). You want a shower? I think Elizabeth will have something to fit, but we'll go to a store if not."

Looking in the mirror, Lauren unbuttoned her denim shirt, took it off and stretched her arm out for Peck to take it.

"On the bed, please?"

She unfastened her bra and handed it to Peck.

"This too?"

Peck tossed them on the bed. Lauren moved toward the tub and unfastened her belt while her right hand turned the bath water on. She glanced at Peck in the doorway. She picked up a box of bubble bath powder and while reading the label asked with a smile:

"Unless you're going to take a bath with me, mind pulling the door?"

Peck stepped into the hall and pulled the door closed.

"Peck?" Lauren asked through the door.

"Hanh?"

"If I doze off, wake me when Elizabeth comes home, please?"

"I will, bébé. You work so hard. You deserve a tub."

28.

BY THE TIME ELIZABETH UNLOCKED THE DOOR and walked in, Peck had been stretched out on the sofa for an hour, reading the seafood and flounder section of one of her cookbooks. Without taking her eyes off Peck, Elizabeth set her bag on the kitchen counter, unbuttoned her chef coat and removed it. She put it on a hanger and hung it on the refrigerator door before she walked to Peck.

"Bonjour mon ami. Être ici me réchauffe le cœur comme si tu étaient ma crème brûlée, mon dessert," Elizabeth said. ("Hello my friend. You being here warms my heart like you're my Creme Brulé, my dessert.")

She knelt on the floor and leaned into him for a kiss. Peck leaned forward and kissed her nipple a friendly hello, sat back and smiled.

"Mon cher," Peck said. "Creme Brulé is crusty, and you know Peck is so sensitive and shy, ha!"

"You are my creme brulé, Peck. Like my dreams of you always. Hard and sweet."

"Cher, you teach Peck what to say from first time we met. You remember when we met?"

"It was 103 degrees, and you walked backward on the sidewalk talking so fast, like a barefoot, silly schoolboy, like you never met a girl before in your life."

"You were the first girl I ever talked too, cher. Ever."

"And I invited you in for some cold water."

"And we sat in your hot bathtub most all night. Oh, cher, we had it all, didn't we?"

"We had everything we ever needed, Peck."

"Ah *oui*."

"Do you think of me?"

"Ever' time I see the moon, cher, I think of my mamma and I think of Elizabeth."

Elizabeth ran her hand up his pantleg, affectionately touching William.

"My dreams of you and our friend here have gotten me through many nights, Boudreaux. I am so happy you are with sweet Millie, but I'll always have you in my heart. Peck, did you have a good reading with Audrey?"

"Ah *oui*."

"So, I shouldn't worry?"

"Nah nah, no worries, cher."

"I wouldn't know what to do if anything ever happened to you. You are my moon."

"Okay, cher. All is good."

Elizabeth leaned and kissed Peck.

"Where's your friend? Is it Lauren?"

"Ah *oui*, she's on the bed. She took a bath and is resting. She's a pedicab girl in New Or-lee-anh, and she works hard saving money for nursing school."

"What's your connection, Peck? Is there a reason you brought her?"

"Dinner, cher. We'll talk at dinner."

"I'll get ready," Elizabeth said.

"Cher, do you have anything Lauren can wear. She's embarrassed she has nothing. We left so fast."

"I'll find something. We're about the same size."

"Cher, Peck is goin' to a store and get some things. Is iced tea okay?"

"Yes, get that and can you get two dozen eggs? I'm out of eggs."

"Ah *oui*."

"Vital Farms. Large."

Peck stepped out of the house as Elizabeth took the hanger and her coat from the refrigerator and went back into the bedroom. Lauren was asleep, lying there in boy's white cotton underwear, hugging a pillow. Elizabeth hung her coat in the closet and stepped over to the bed and gently touched Lauren's calf.

"Huh?" Lauren muttered, waking up.

"Hi Lauren, it's me, Elizabeth."

"Baton Rouge?" Lauren mumbled.

"*Oui*," Elizabeth said. "Baton Rouge."

Lauren sat up as Elizabeth switched the bedside lamp on. Next to the lamp rested Peck's phone. There was a Tarot card resting on his phone. *The Hanged Man* card.

"What's this card for?"

"Audrey gave it to him because he turned it. She thinks it's a destiny for traffickers."

"*Merde*," Elizabeth said. "Peck never forgets his phone. Something's distracting him."

"Where did Peck go?" Lauren asked.

"He went to get some eggs and iced tea. He'll be back soon."

"Oh?"

"I'm to dress you for a French dining experience this evening. You look my size, may I try?"

"You don't mind?"

Elizabeth stood and began to open closet doors.

"Lauren, is Peck working on something? I know he does things for Lily Cup, the attorney, but whenever he thinks there's trouble, he comes and has his cards read."

"Our secret?" Lauren asked.

"Of course."

"He's trying to save a girl."

"*Excusez-moi*?"

"A little girl who was kidnapped when she was nine."

"*Oh mon seigneur.*" ("Oh, my lord.")

"She was sold into slavery. Now she's thirteen."

Tears filled Elizabeth's eyes.

"I promised to help him, but don't worry. He told me that now there's a secret phone number to text whenever a girl was in trouble like that, and that's all I know so far, but the secret number does something good, I heard. It takes care of it or something," Lauren said.

Peck's phone rang.

"That's Millie," Elizabeth said. "I should answer."

"He told me about Millie," Lauren said.

"Hi Millie, this is Elizabeth, how are you?"

"How did—? Are you in—?" Millie stuttered.

"Peck came up to see Audrey to read his Tarot cards. Minutes ago he ran out to get some iced tea and he forgot to take his phone. Has he mentioned my graduation?"

"Not yet, but he's had a lot on his mind. I'm sure he will. Can we come to it?"

"But of course. I sent you invitations."

"Oh good. I'm so worried Peck was doing something dangerous for Lily Cup. He investigates for her. If you find out if he's in danger will you tell me?"

"Not to worry, Millie. I learned he has a secret phone number to text whenever somebody sees something bad."

Lauren held her index finger over her mouth as if to "shhh."

"Has he told you about the little girl?" Millie asked.

"Oh, *oui*— so sad. I've heard."

"Breaks my heart people can be so cruel," Millie said. "I want to help too."

"It has to be a secret, Millie. You can't tell Peck I told you about a phone number."

"I promise. I think Gabe is helping him. He told me about a girl a man was beating and making do things."

"I didn't know you knew, Millie."

"Only a little. He told me some. My Civics paper is on Sex Trafficking. Don't tell Peck, I want to surprise him."

"I won't."

"Due tomorrow. You wouldn't believe the sites I've found online for my research. I found a site where a man is selling sex with a pregnant girl, in Louisiana. Can you imagine, Elizabeth?"

"Merde," Elizabeth said as she lifted the Tarot card Peck left on his phone. "He should be hung."

"She's going to have a baby," Millie said, "and he's selling her body."

"The Hanged Man," Elizabeth said, looking at the card in her hand.

"Hang him?"

"No, *The Hanged Man*. It's a Tarot Card. It would be perfect to hang that bastard," Elizabeth said.

"I just looked it up—*The Hanged Man*," Millie said. "Good title for my paper. Can you imagine what he's putting that girl through?"

"Unfortunately, I can. It's so sad."

"See you at graduation, Elizabeth. Congratulations."

"See you soon, Millie. I'll tell Peck you called."

Elizabeth ended the call and set the phone down.

"Please be honest with me, Lauren. Is Peck in serious trouble?" Elizabeth asked.

"I promise he's not," Lauren said. "He's only trying to do a good thing."

Elizabeth seemed contented with that.

"*Bon*! So, let's get you dressed."

"You don't mind?"

"What's your mood tonight *belle fille*, are you in a casual satin buttoned blouse mood or are we in that *I want all eyes on me just for walking into the room* mood?" Elizabeth teased.

"*Looking at me* would be nice."

"Me too," Elizabeth said. "Let's do it."

Lauren grinned.

"We'll turn heads, *n'est pas*?" Elizabeth asked.

"I dress like a boy because I have to pedal a bike all day taking people around like they're royalty."

Lauren stood up.

"Look at my knees. They're scratched and bruised like a schoolboy. Look at this disgusting underwear! I have to wear two pair of these boy's cotton underwear or my ass will chaff and my crotch gets sore."

Elizabeth knelt and stripped Lauren's boy's underwear down to the floor.

"We'll start with lingerie, *mon cherie*."

She got up, pulled a drawer open, took panties from it and tossed them on the bed.

"Pick your pleasure," Elizabeth said. "They'll fit."

Lauren picked two panties up.

"My bra is nude color. Which of these will go best?"

Elizabeth walked to Lauren, her hands out.

"May I, cher?"

Lauren nodded as Elizabeth gently pressed her open palms on Lauren's breasts.

"These are not boys, *mon cherie*. These are definitely girls."

Lauren grinned.

"You need no bra, *belle fille*, such a beautiful body. I never wear a bra. Pick any color you like."

Before they went out for an evening of celebrating old and new friendships, Lauren was dressed to the nines in a black satin full midcalf skirt with black, thigh-high stockings and black panties. Her top was an ivory deep V neck satin with a pewter coin hanging on the chain just at her hint of cleavage. She looked amazing.

Elizabeth applied Lauren's makeup as if she was about to go onstage. Elizabeth looked devastatingly Parisian as well. Clamando, of course, in a lace-hemmed slip skirt with side slit. Peck got to wear a new dark satin shirt with black pearl buttons that Elizabeth was holding for his birthday.

The candle on a corner table at the Bistro was lighted and burgundy napkins of Egyptian cotton rested on three polished brass plates. The evening began with gentle toasts to old times and new ones and of far-off friends, Millie and Lily Cup and Gabe and Sasha, Peck's family forever. They talked of beef bourguignon and of escargot. Of where the scalloped potato was first created— in England. They spoke of tartare, and Peck was mesmerized as he watched raw egg yolks getting smashed into anchovies and a two-foot-tall pepper mill. There was a warm glow about their table. The ladies were exquisite and Elizabeth would kick a heel off under the table and nestle her foot on Peck's inner thigh to make a point that her memories of their being there for each other had never subsided. Elizabeth asked Lauren if she liked crepes and jams for breakfast, or would she prefer a coddled egg. Lauren broke into tears, only for a moment, believing she was in a dream.

"Why the tears? Are you sad?" Elizabeth asked.

"I'm sad for girls who can't have a normal life like this," Lauren said.

"Lauren and I are working on something to help a girl, cher. They call it trafficking," Peck said.

"I'm scared, but I'm helping Peck. We want to help a girl escape, but then I'm going back to school."

"School?" Elizabeth asked.

"Nursing school. I need one more year. I'll do that and thinking maybe I'll go on and be a veterinarian."

"That would be good, dass for true," Peck said.

"I promise to stay until we get Tiffany safe, but then back to school. I've almost saved enough."

Peck lifted his wine glass.

"To Tiffany and to nurse Lauren," he said.

They all toasted.

The trafficking issue they had driven away from was only mentioned in this passing. It was almost as if they didn't want to spoil a grand evening with the real world. On one of Elizabeth's visits to the ladies room, Peck told Lauren he was thinking of an idea to pass the word of the secret phone number to the pedicab drivers, so trapped girls and boys might get saved. If they could get the slaves to tell the hotels and room numbers of whoever paid for their sex, the police, even days and weeks later, they could trace who rented the room and reprimand them for contributing to the problem of buying sex and financing the sex slavery market.

After a Grand Marnier souffle, Peck, Elizabeth and Lauren strolled home, chatting, laughing, and pointing at the stars. At the apartment Peck encouraged the girls to stay dressed as they were beautiful, and the night was a catch-up celebration for holidays and birthdays and other times Elizabeth and he never got to see each other.

Elizabeth poured brandy snifters while Peck sat on the floor, leaning back on the sofa admiring the beauty. It was late when Elizabeth handed the goblets as a nightcap and sat on the front edge of the sofa next to Peck. Lauren casually paraded around in the living room and kitchen, enjoying seeing her reflections in mirrors and from the glass in picture frames.

"Tu pourrais être un modèle, une telle beauté que tu es, fille," Elizabeth said. ("You could be a model, such a beauty you are, girl.")

Lauren smiled at recognizing a couple of the French words, and she walked over to Elizabeth and lifted her skirt a tad, exposing her stockings and bare thighs with a stage-like curtsy and held her snifter out for a click. They clicked and sipped.

"Isn't Lauren lovely, Peck?"

"Inside and out," Peck said. "She's—how you say—good people."

"I feel like I was at my prom, thank you both. I'm excited that I'm going back to school, after …"

"You're the guest. You may have the bed to yourself or this sofa, which opens out and is closer to the kitchen. Your choice," Elizabeth said.

"The sofa is fine with me."

Peck and Elizabeth stood.

"Toss the dress and things on that chair. The panties are my gift. They've never been worn before tonight."

Elizabeth lifted her skirt with a smile, showing she was without panties. Lauren laughed.

"Please use the bathroom. It won't bother us. And in this house brassieres and tops are optional," Elizabeth said.

"Me too?" Peck mused.

"Especially you, you sexy man," Elizabeth said with a grin.

They all joined a group hug.

Peck and Elizabeth started down the hall.

"Night, and thank you again," Lauren said.

"Night frien'," Peck said.

Peck and Elizabeth stripped in the dark and fell into bed as they had done so many times before. They held each other tenderly, as friends, not as lovers, but kissed warmly with slow kisses looking into each other's eyes as they nestled. Elizabeth held William passively with gentle hands, stroking with her fingertips. Peck's fingernails scratched affectionate lazy circles on the base of Elizabeth's spine with the occasional journey down her butt crack and then she would kiss his cheek a *thank you.*

"What time is it, cher?" Peck asked.

"2:37, why?"

"We should go, Elizabeth."

"Can't you sleep?"

"I've got to get back and Lauren could be earning money in the morning with her pedicab."

Knowing her dearest friend had so much on his mind, Elizabeth jumped out of bed and went to the kitchen.

With every light in the living room and kitchen turned on, Elizabeth stood topless in the kitchen, wearing her chef hat and preparing English muffins with melted French butter and orange marmalade, coddled eggs with chives and white pepper. Peck and Lauren ate standing up and reminisced about their night at the Bistro and the fun they had. The topless at home routine started for Elizabeth during her early days at cooking school. One morning she spilled orange juice and stained her heavily starched white chef's cooking coat and that stain got her a demerit and lower grade for the day.

Peck and Lauren paid no notice to her ritual and laughed and spoke of the food and wine from the night before, and how fun it was to dress up in this new world that doesn't respect propriety. Lauren mentioned how beautiful she felt wearing stockings that covered the scratches and bruises on her knees. They spoke of a world that had somehow convinced itself that trying to make a good impression and feeling good about one's self was an offense to personal liberty and freedom. *It's like not having to make your bed in the morning,* Gabe would say. *In the army, you still have to make your bed.*

Big hugs all around with promises to return, Peck and Lauren got in the pickup, and by 3:49 a.m. they were driving toward New Orleans.

<h1>29.</h1>

EIGHTY MILES AWAY FROM BATON ROUGE, in Covington, a suburb of New Orleans, the phone on Lieutenant Larry Gaines's bedside table lit up. The lieutenant coughed a husky morning throat clearing, clutched the phone and answered it.

"It's after three. This better be good," Larry said.

"Officer Landry, Lieutenant," Officer Landry said.

"What's up?" Larry asked.

"Gert Town," Officer Landry's voice crackled.

"Gert Town? This can't be good," Larry grumbled.

Officer Landry gave the name of a Gert Town motel and its address.

"What's the trouble?" Larry asked, standing up.

"Chief's been here and gone, Lieutenant. He told me to call you, said this has your name all over it, and to wake you up."

"Don't tell me. A blow to the forehead, right?"

"Not sure about anything, Lieutenant. I just got here. Coroner is on his way."

"Well, why the hell did the chief tell you to wake me up? He must have seen something."

"I'm no expert, Lieutenant, but I'd say it looks like torture."

"Torture?"

"Yes, sir."

"What's with all the noise?"

"It's pouring here, Lieutenant."

"Cover the body, Officer, until Chris gets there."

"I can't do that, Lieutenant."

"That's an order, Landry."

"But I can't do it, sir."

"This better be good, Landry. Why can't you do it?"

"This guy's hanging, Lieutenant. He's been hanged."

"Black man? Lynching?" Larry queried.

"He's a white man, Lieutenant."

"I'm on my way. Don't touch a thing."

That 3:45 a.m. had a full moon, but it was raining and rain with lightning under a full moon was bad *gris-gris* to begin with, and heavy rain like this in New Orleans didn't let up until it was good and ready. Larry made his way into Gert Town, the empty belly of New Orleans poverty, the city so poor and down it had to stand on its tiptoes to look up at sea level.

The neighborhood looked like a Great Depression Hooverville. Larry lifted his 12-gauge shotgun from its stand on the dash and rested it on the seat beside him. There were few sidewalks in this part of town, and hospitality here was pay-by-the-hour motels. He saw flashing lights of police cars. He counted six of them and the two driving in his direction. He came to a stop in the middle of the street. A patrol officer flagged him a signal that he'd stand watch over his car. Larry pulled his trench coat collar up and walked in pouring rain to the parking area of the two-story motel that looked as if it was out of an early 1950s movie.

The headlights of a police car parked sideways illuminated a body hanging upside down from a wrought iron railing on the second floor. No onlookers had gathered. Gert Town was dangerous at this hour.

"A pretty fancy hanging, Sergeant. Look at how he's been tied. It is a man, isn't it?"

"It's a man, Lieutenant, and it does have some fancy rope work."

"What do we have so far?" Larry asked.

"Not much. Just got here when I called you."

"What have you done so far?"

"Lieutenant, I've stationed officers around the place. We haven't let anyone come in or leave. All I know is the man is dead. There was no pulse on his neck. I had to get the Fire Safety guys to ladder up to it to verify."

"You've done well, Sergeant. Have the front desk pull the plug on the room phones."

"Will do, Lieutenant. Most people use iPhones these days."

"So, if they have wi-fi, have them unplug that."

"Yes sir."

"Have you heard from Chris?"

"Coroner O'Sullivan is on his way, Lieutenant."

"Let's go upstairs and have a look," Larry said.

The body, a Caucasian, male, was clothed and hung upside down. From a ground vantage point he appeared to be hanging by his ankles from the second-floor balcony railing. His head was pulled backward. Larry and Officer Landry started up the steps.

"We're going to need a lady detective, Sergeant," Larry said. "A full detective. We're going to go room by room, and I'll need female backup."

"Yes sir, I'll make a call."

"When she gets here, knock on every door, Sergeant. Tell everyone to be patient. It's going to be a long night. If there are any medical needs, have paramedics to stand by."

"Yes sir."

"Let's see if the owners of this Taj Mahal or any of the front desk staff know the victim, or heard or saw anything."

"Lieutenant, I think this is a place where they're paid not to see or hear anything."

"Welcome to the Big Easy, bébé," Larry said. "Sergeant, remind them the penalties for lying to a cop."

"I will, sir."

"Who discovered the body, Sergeant?"

"A drive-by called 911, Lieutenant. They wanted to stay anonymous. They called from a pay phone."

"Get a copy of the call for voice ID."

"Yes sir."

Larry walked to the rail just above the hanging body. He pointed at bands of rope banded around one ankle.

"See that, Sergeant?"

"I see it, sir."

"What do you make of it?"

"It looks like he's tied with new cotton clothesline rope, Lieutenant."

"Look how he's tied, Sergeant. This took somebody some time. He's got one ankle wrapped a bunch of times. It's a neat wrap. It's not just slung around his ankle. That's the one connected to the railing—"

"Only one ankle. I see it, Lieutenant."

"The other ankle is tied with the same rope, wrapped exactly like this one but that ankle is hanging down and away from this ankle."

"Yes sir."

"I don't get it."

"Maybe it slipped, Lieutenant?"

"That foot didn't slip, Sergeant."

Sergeant Landry leaned over to look.

"I think whoever did this meant for it to hang just the way it looks," Larry said.

"It could be, sir."

"I think it's a message," Larry said.

"I wouldn't have a clue, Lieutenant."

"This is Gert Town, Sergeant. This is the N'Orleans we hide from the world; French and Spanish pirates would go into the bars to out-drink their targets and shanghai them. They'd carry them blind drunk to ships in port waiting to set sail. They'd get away with it walking through streets of echoing jazz, bar brawls and the laughter of full-breasted ladies of the evening—the night sounds. The days here were quiet and camouflaged by trucks from manufacturing plants that filled glass jars with mayonnaise and little green nickel bottles with Coca Cola, blocking its dirty underwear. Gert Town's a boil on Pelican City's ass, Sergeant."

"It's another world, Lieutenant."

"So, what do we have? We've got a full moon, we've got lightning, we've got a stiff hanging by one heel."

"Not a lot to go on in the rain, Lieutenant."

"We need a brother, Sergeant," Larry said.

"Excuse me, sir?"

"Are there any brothers here?"

"Lieutenant, are you referring to a black officer?"

"Preferably a young one, Sergeant."

"Isn't that a bit racist, Lieutenant? Internal Affairs could have a field day with it."

Larry looked at the sergeant with exasperation, as if he shouldn't have to explain that colloquial in the heart of New Orleans to any N'Orleans cop. He held his chocolate brown hand up for the sergeant to see his skin color.

"I need a young one, Sergeant."

"Yes sir."

"I need someone tuned in to today's world."

The sergeant pressed a button on his two-way and asked by name for an officer to come up. A young cadet in training came up the stairs and to the scene.

"You called, Sergeant?"

"Deputy Aguillard, Lieutenant Gaines here asked for you."

"For me?"

"You Creole, son?" Larry asked.

"I'm sure I am somewhere, sir. I have four uncles that talk about Creole, sir."

"Deputy, I need a brother to look at something."

"Look at what, exactly, sir?"

"Everything around us. I need you to look it over, Deputy. Tell me if anything speaks to you."

"Yes sir, Lieutenant."

The cadet leaned down and examined the tied ankles, one at a time. He got down on one knee. He studied the different knots, the way the rope was one long strand and not several pieces of rope tied together. He knelt on the other side and studied the corpse's arms behind his back and how the hands were tied. The cadet stood up and stepped back.

"Pretty sure that's voodoo, Lieutenant."

"Is that your opinion, Deputy?"

"No sir, it's voodoo, sir. Pretty sure."

"Talk to me, brother. Take me through it."

"See how he's hanging, Lieutenant?"

"Talk to me."

"It's *The Hanged Man* card, Lieutenant."

"The Hanged Man?"

The deputy stood back out of the rain and searched his phone for an image and showed it to Larry.

"You know about Tarot, Lieutenant?"

"Not much."

"*The Hanged Man*—it's a Tarot sign, Lieutenant. If you pull *The Hanged Man* card with a reader it could mean the ultimate surrender. I don't believe in voodoo myself, Lieutenant, but my gramma talks to her Tarot cards all the time. That's how I know about it. She has bad arthritis and sometimes I have to shuffle them for her. *The Hanged Man* is the ultimate surrender."

"Looks pretty ultimate to me, Deputy."

"It means sacrifice, being suspended in time, sir."

"Are you suggesting it's self-inflicted, a suicide?"

"Can I look closer, Lieutenant?"

"Be my guest, Deputy."

"Could a man tie himself up like that? He'd need help, wouldn't he?" Larry asked.

The cadet lowered his eye level to that of the second-floor railing. He studied every inch of the rail near the ropes connected to it.

"Here we go," the deputy said.

"What?"

"I think it's murder, not suicide."

"Talk to me, Deputy."

"I found the *tell*, Lieutenant."

"What'd you find?"

"Lean in here, sir."

The cadet pointed his flashlight on the rail just next to the ropes that wrapped it.

"Can you see it, Lieutenant?"

"Barely, in the rain, but I see something. What is it?"

"It's fishing line, Lieutenant. It's tied separately to the railing. That's fishing line they use on those expensive offshore fishing charters. It's tied to the rail, out of sight. They used black line to hide it."

"What do you make of it, Deputy?"

"If my hunch is right, Lieutenant, this man has been murdered and the murderer is sending a message."

"What's your hunch, Deputy?"

"Can I run downstairs, sir? I need to see something."

"Be my guest, Deputy."

Standing on the ground under the hanging body, the cadet yelled up.

"I'm right, Lieutenant. Pretty sure this was murder."

He ran up the stairs and back over to the lieutenant.

"Talk to me, Deputy."

"That same fishing line was tied around his neck. It's pretty dark on his neck so it looks like it's wound several times around, and it's pulling his head back. They used black so you couldn't see it too quickly here on the rail, but my guess is fishing line strangled him or broke his neck, killing him. My guess, sir, is that if it was suicide, he'd a just hanged himself straight up."

"I'm impressed, Deputy."

"Thank you, sir."

"You say they're sending a message, son. What makes you think that?"

"Lieutenant, you want to kill a man today, you pull a gun and toast him. Whoever did this put on a Hollywood show. There has to be a reason, sir. They posed this man's body as a Tarot card, in one of the most superstitious cities in the world."

"Good eyes, my brother."

"Look at this, Lieutenant," the sergeant said, pointing to the fishing line tied to the railing. "I think the deputy is on to something."

"What?"

"See this double knot tied in the fishing line, sir?"

"I do."

"This knot was right at the side of the rail. I'll bet they measured it before they tossed this guy over and knew how long it had to be to choke him or to break his neck, sir," the sergeant said.

"Maybe," Larry said.

"The rope looped a few times around his neck could tell us something else too, Lieutenant," the deputy said.

"Tell us what?"

"I think he was dead before they dropped him over."

"Talk to me, Deputy."

"I think they took their time in a room to dress up the ropes pretty—him dead all along. Then they drop him over."

"And the fishing line is fastened here to make it look like it broke his neck," the sergeant said.

"Probably did break his neck, Sergeant, but my guess is he was already dead," the deputy said.

"Coroner O'Sullivan will tell us," Landry said.

"Good work, both of you," Larry said.

His radio squawked.

"Lieutenant?"

"Copy."

"Lieutenant, Officer Downs here. Can I come up?"

"Copy. What'cha got, Downs?"

"I need to come up, Lieutenant."

"Copy. C'mon up."

Officer Downs came up to the second floor and over to Larry.

"I wanted to keep this quiet, Lieutenant."

"Talk to me."

"It's somethin' we found. Out back."

"This can't be good."

"Yes sir."

"Spare the drama, Officer. What did you find behind this palace?"

"Bodies, sir."

"Did you say body or bodies?"

"That's with an *s*, sir. Bodies. In the dumpster."

"How many?"

"We don't know yet."

"And so it begins," Larry said.

"Lieutenant, they're stacked like pancakes. Haven't touched them. We're waiting on the coroner."

"We're going to need a bigger morgue," Larry mused.

"Sir, I think our morgue can—"

"I'm joking, Downs. It's from a movie—"

"Oh."

"—before you were born."

"Okay, sir. I didn't want to announce it for ears, sir."

"Good thinking, Officer. Keep a lid on it, and the dumpster— put a guard on it. Broaden the perimeter around the property, close the street. Nobody gets in or out. The murderer could still be here."

"There's something else, Lieutenant."

"Talk to me."

"We could only see two faces, but they looked like they had brands on their foreheads."

"Brands?"

"They looked like Roman numerals, sir."

Larry touched his cell phone and put it to his ear.

"Carol, wake a judge up. I need search warrants."

"Warrants for where, Lieutenant?" Carol asked.

"For every room at this Taj Mahal in Gert Town— every room. I want warrants by room number."

"One for every room, sir?"

"I don't need a bunch of New Orleans 'miss the forest for the trees' law students pulling bullshit about illegal search and seizures, citizen's rights in a city whose daily newspaper runs two full pages of advertising for handguns like they're tomatoes and radishes on pages two and three. I'm covering my ass on this one, Carol. Sergeant Landry is going to call you in about two seconds. Listen carefully, and I need the warrants here pronto."

Larry ended the call and turned to Landry.

"Landry, you heard me. Call Carol and don't miss a room. I have a feeling we're going to find some surprises in this toilet."

Larry turned to Officer Downs.

"Officer Downs, why are you still here? Secure the dumpster. If this is voodoo, it's going to be a long night. The moon is full. Better get a move on!"

"Yes sir."

Larry tapped him on the shoulder.

"Downs?"

"Yes sir?"

"Take Deputy Aguillard with you. Let him look."

"Yes sir."

"Deputy, report to me after."

"Yes, Lieutenant."

The Orleans Parish coroner drove in and took over managing the crime scene. The hanged man was cut down and bagged. Four bodies were lifted from the dumpster, bagged, and taken to the morgue, along with the hanged man.

A lady detective and Larry with valid search warrants began pounding on one room door at a time. In the third room they visited, a pregnant girl in her teens cowered on the floor next to a bed. She was naked, with a towel wrapped around her.

"Get out!" she screamed.

"We're police, we have a warrant," the lady detective said.

"Get out!"

"Do you have a license or ID?"

"I don't have to talk to you."

"Just your identification," the lady detective said.

"Roger told me never to talk to cops."

"I just need—"

"I don't have to talk to cops. Don't ever trust cops."

"Do you have a license or other identification?"

The girl turned her head away.

"How far along are you?" the lady detective asked.

"Seven months."

"You must be hungry, sweetheart. Are you hungry?" the lady detective asked.

"Yes."

"Show me an ID and we'll get you some food."

"I can't."

"Can't or you won't?"

"I can't."

"Why can't you?"

"I don't have any."

"You don't have an ID or driver's license?"

"Roger keeps all of that safe. He protects me. We're getting married … and I'm seventeen. Yesterday was my birthday. Roger gave me those roses. Aren't they beautiful? They're Tyler roses and they're magical. Roger wants me to hold them when we get married Saturday."

As Detective Gaines was leaning on the door to give the female detective her space to work with the girl, his phone lit up.

"Chris, what'cha got?" he whispered.

"Lieutenant, four male bodies, each strangled with a garrote. Heavy-weight fishing line around their necks so fine they couldn't undo it with their fingers. My guess is they were somehow tossed in the dumpster alive and they suffocated from a garrote choke. The Roman numerals XII are carved into their foreheads. This was an old-world assassination, Lieutenant. I haven't seen it in years."

"Lab work?"

"Still on it, Lieutenant, but one thing certain, all four victims had sperm on their genitals. Each victim had their own room at the motel. Forensic is pulling DNA from sheets, pillows, and towels."

"And our friend, the Christmas tree ornament?"

"A Roger Stillman, Lake Charles, Louisiana. Age thirty-one, a mile-long rap sheet of petty crimes. A con man. He was dead from choking, garrote style. Dropped over the rail and suffered a broken neck post mortem."

"What do you mean broken neck post mortem?"

"He was dead two hours before they dropped him."

"Spectacular work, my friend. I'll be over today."

Larry turned his phone to silent and interrupted the lady detective with the pregnant girl.

"Young lady, I'm arresting you—suspicion of soliciting prostitution."

"I don't have to talk to you."

"You have the right to remain silent. Anything you say can be used against you in court. You have a right to talk to a lawyer before we ask you any questions. You have the right to have a lawyer with you during questioning. If you cannot afford a lawyer, one will be appointed for you before any questioning, if you wish. If you decide to answer questions now without a lawyer present, you have the right to stop answering at any time. Do you understand the rights I have just read to you?"

"Shut up."

"With these rights in mind, do you wish to speak to me?"

"I don't have to talk to you. Roger will—"

"Do you understand the rights I just read to you?"

"Yes, but it doesn't matter, Roger—"

"Roger is dead, young lady."

"No!" the girl screamed.

"Someone took care of your Roger a few hours ago in the rain. Detective, handcuff her, take her in. Hold her for questioning."

"Yes, Lieutenant."

She motioned for the girl to stand.

"Let's get you dressed, sweetie."

"Let me make something clear, young lady," Larry said.

"What?" the girl asked in tears.

"I don't want your baby born in prison, and that's what's about to happen if you don't cooperate. You can get two years for prostitution."

"You can't arrest me. I'm not old enough."

"Two days ago, maybe, but you're seventeen now, and that's legal age in Louisiana."

"So why are you arresting me if you don't want my baby born in prison?"

"The detective here is taking you in for questioning. We need your help finding who murdered Roger. You help us and we'll let you go, no charges of prostitution."

"But I don't know anything, Roger never—"

"Did he put you here?"

"Yes."

"Did he promise if you had sex with strangers—?"

"And you'll let me go if I help?"

"We will let you go."

"Roger would tell me to get a lawyer."

"Money pretty tight?" Larry asked.

"We were buying a house. We were getting married in our new back yard. Saturday."

"Honey, a criminal attorney will cost you ten grand, more as you go."

"I can't afford that."

"Yes, you can."

"I can?"

"How many days and nights have you been working this motel?" Larry asked.

"So far five days and nights, I think. I'm supposed to stay here until Saturday, when we get married. Roger was in another room with his computer, getting me guys. I have to go to their rooms and do them. Roger tells me what to wear."

"Roger had $20,500 in cash in his pocket."

"That's for our house."

"You want it for a house, or do you want to give it to an attorney?"

"A house or apartment for my baby."

"It's your money."

"Really?" The girl wept.

"Roger had something else in his pocket."

"My ring?"

"No ring. He had a single one-way ticket for a Roger Stillman to Acapulco, Mexico. Saturday morning at 9:35, Aeromexico."

The girl put her hands on her stomach as if she was letting tears wash away her dreams.

"Has he put you up in motels before?"

"In Houston, for two days. I did four guys. Beaumont once, one guy."

"He was running out on you. He was using you. He only cared about himself. Saturday morning, he wasn't going to marry anybody. He was taking the money, boarding a plane and leaving you and your baby stranded and on your own."

The lady detective put her arm around the girl.

"You knew it, didn't you, sweetie?" the lady detective asked. "You knew it all along. You just didn't want to believe it."

The girl sobbed in her arms.

"He promised he would take care of our baby."

"Detective, after this is over, see that our friend and her baby get every penny of the money," Larry said.

"My name's Priscilla."

"Detective, treat Priscilla, our momma-to-be to a good breakfast. Stay with her. Let her do some filing help around your office, maybe. Keep her close to you. I'll be in for questioning after I make some rounds."

"Handcuffs?" Priscilla asked.

"No handcuffs."

Priscilla smiled through tears.

"Lieutenant, I'll keep her busy," the lady detective said.

"And take your time taking her in, Detective. Let our friend have a good long soak in a hot tub. Keep her safe."

"I will, Lieutenant. She's in good hands."

"Priscilla, you're safe now. It's over. No more being used, if you learn from it. The detective here is a momma of four, and she'll have ideas about where you can get help."

"Thank you."

30.

LARRY WAS VISIBLY SHAKEN.

As he walked to his car, he called Chris O'Sullivan, the coroner.

"Yes, Lieutenant?"

"Our Christmas ornament has been pimping out a seventeen-year-old girl since she was fifteen. Turned seventeen yesterday, pregnant. He's been hooking her all week in that dump, no telling what she's been through."

"Our Roger Stillman?" O'Sullivan asked.

"Our Roger Stillman."

"Looking at Mr. Stillman as we speak, Lieutenant. He's all choked up."

"Cute, Chris. I needed a laugh."

"What a morning, Lieutenant. How can I help?"

"I want you to mark his file: Sex Trafficker."

"I'll make a note of it on his file."

"Get a rubber stamp. SEX TRAFFICKER stamped on every page. It's time the country gets its head out of its ass and recognizes how big a problem this is, and in a lot of the cases it starts with someone these kids know and think they can trust."

"I'll order one today, Lieutenant."

"Get a big one, Chris."

"I'll pick it out personally, Lieutenant."

"She believed he was going to marry her on Saturday morning. He gave her a ten dollar bunch of roses from a street vendor and had her convinced that if she sexed fifteen-twenty guys a day for a week with anything they wanted, they'd buy a house for the baby, get married Saturday and live happily ever after."

"And she bought it, Lieutenant."

"And all he bought was a one-way ride to Acapulco," Larry said.

"Want to know what I think, Lieutenant?"

"You're the only voice I trust, Chris. Talk to me."

"What kind of lawyer would defend somebody like Christmas ornament here? How low can they get?"

"Some fat politician turned *low* into *law*, Chris and there you have it. Some prick turned *lower* into *lawyer*."

"It's like the attorneys want to keep the vermin on the streets making money, Lieutenant, so they can pay legal fees."

"Christmas ornament is a nobody, Chris. A small-time grifter. Who would go to such elaborate means to hang him out to dry like that? The way he was tied was an art form. It had to be premeditated."

"The report says officer Downs found Stillman's computer," Lieutenant. "He had a website selling sex with an innocent, underage, lactating, pregnant schoolgirl. My guess is an undercover vigilante followed them into Gert Town, found his room and sucker-punched him. Let's see if pix of the body hanging appear on the web anywhere. Wouldn't be surprised."

"I've got to eat."

"Go home, Lieutenant. Get some rest."

31.

WHILE PECK DROVE and he and Lauren talked about the night and how they had to come up with a game plan to organize pedicab drivers and a way to get the sex slaves to cry for help, Lily Cup had spent a sleepless night and was at home sitting on the edge of her bed, texting Lieutenant Larry Gaines.

"Satanic murders in Gert Town? Larry, is that any way to wake a lady? Have you got anything to do with the morning news, big guy?" Lily Cup asked.

Almost as quickly as she sent the text, Larry called her. She answered with, "Are you in Gert Town?"

"Since three a.m."

"You okay, Larry?"

"You a Billie Holliday fan?"

"I love Billie Holliday," Lily Cup said.

"In clubs Billie would sing a song with her eyes closed. Leave the stage and never do an encore."

In his deepest bass Larry sang into the phone.

"Southern trees bear a strange fruit.

Blood on the leaves and blood at the root,

Black bodies swinging in the southern breeze,

Strange fruit hanging from the poplar trees."

"Damn," Lily Cup said. "That's heavy."

"It reminded her of her father dying young of a lung disorder after being turned away from a hospital because he was a black man. If she was in a club and sang it, all service would stop to listen," Larry said.

"Was this guy black? A lynching?"

"No on black. Not sure on lynching."

"Was he hung, like radio news reported?"

"Upside down by his ankles and choked to death."

"What kind of animals are we?" Lily Cup asked.

Larry didn't respond.

"You must be exhausted."

"I could use a tub."

"This girl got no court today. What say I run a tub for my favorite Lieutenant and he bring some brown sugar for a soak?"

"Tempting."

"Bananas Foster French Toast and Creole rice cakes inspire you?"

"Had I'd known you could put that dog on, I'd a made your place a regular stop long ago."

"Imagine l'il ol' me, a Lieutenant Larry booty call, be still my heart," Lily Cup said. She laughed.

"Give a brother banana foster toast and he'll follow you anywhere," Larry quipped.

"I can't lie, I order in, but they deliver warm."

"I'm tempted."

"C'mon over. Let's give the Garden District something to talk about. Enough with Satanic headlines before breakfast."

"On my way."

Lily Cup dialed Peck's number twice. The first time she was messaged that he couldn't answer as he was driving. Thirty minutes later she called him again. Peck's phone was ringing as he drove. He saw it was Lily Cup. He looked over at Lauren. He held a finger up, signaling not to speak as he touched the Bluetooth button on his steering wheel.

"How you are, cher?"

"Where are you, Peck?"

"Oh cher, you should see what they done to my swamps and the Maurepas— why they chop all them pretty cypress trees?"

"Are you driving?"

"Ah *oui*."

"Peck, is your radio on?"

"Nah nah."

"Have you been listening to the news? Television? Anything?"

"Where's wild turkeys and wood ducks goin' to go, cher? No cypress trees, no more seeds, no more squirrels."

"Peck! Stay focused. Have you heard the news?"

The tracker in Peck cautioned him to parse his words, to hold his thoughts in for critical moments. A secret to tracking was listening and watching.

"No cher, why?"

"Where were you at 3:00 a.m. Peck?"

"Hanh?"

"3:00 a.m.— where were you?"

"I was in Baton Rouge with Elizabeth, cher, and my good frien' Lauren. Ah *oui*."

"Where are you now?"

"I'm driving to New Or-lee-anh. Oh, we pass a good time in Baton Rouge, cher—Elizabeth say hi. I had tartare, first time ever."

"Did you see Audrey for a reading?"

"Saw Audrey, ah *oui*. Want me to come over when I get there?"

"Not this morning, Peck, just go home. I'll text you later. Maybe we can do Charlie's tonight."

"What you going to tell me about the radio?"

"Nothing, Peck. Just go home, I'll call you later."

"Okay, cher. Bye."

Peck pushed the Bluetooth button to *off*.

"Peck, do you remember the first time we talked and you asked me to help you find Tiffany?" Lauren asked.

"Ah *oui*, bébé, I remember."

"You said you'd Zydeco with me. I know we haven't found her, but think maybe we can dance tonight?"

"Ah, sure, bébé. We go to Mulate's and dance, dass for true. Two to the left, two to the right. We pass a good time tonight, bébé. I'll pick you up."

"It was fun in Baton Rouge, dressing up and going out. I just want to be held by someone. Sorry if that's silly."

"Nah nah, bébé, never silly to hold somebody. We dance good tonight, we hold good."

As Lily Cup was getting dressed in anticipation of Larry's stopping by, Peck was dropping Lauren at her apartment. He drove home from there and found Gabe sitting with a morning newspaper, sipping chicory.

"How you are, Gabe?"

"My brother."

"Elizabeth said hello to you."

"Is that woman still as beautiful?"

"Ah *oui*, dass for true. She graduates in a month. Ain't that somethin'?"

"A full chef, just imagine. That's her ticket around the world, son."

"She said she's moving to Paris."

"It poured last night, my brother. St. Charles looked more than a foot or two deep this morning. It was draining about an hour ago when I went for my walk. How was your drive in?"

"No rain in Baton Rouge, but I had tartare first time."

"Oh my. Steak or salmon, son?"

"Salmon, that was it. I saw 'em make it. Egg yolk, capers, anchovies. Gabe, it was something."

Gabe held up the newspaper with a picture of the motel. The picture had been taken in the daylight and there was one police car parked in front of it but no images of bodies.

"Look at the news, son. *Murders in Gert Town.*"

"This is New Or-lee-anhs, Gabe."

"Says it happened last night."

"Drugs, ya think, Gabe?"

"Nobody's talking until they find next of kin, but says here, five dead."

"Aye-yi-yi," Peck said.

"They're predicting a satanic ritual, but being closed-mouthed about it."

"Gabe, I saw Audrey in Baton Rouge, and now I need your help with something, okay?"

"For a reading, son?"

"Ah *oui*."

"Pour a coffee and sit. I'm all ears."

Peck filled Gabe's cup, poured one for himself and took the pot back into the kitchen.

"Gabe, on what we're working on, the slave thing, we need to come up with some way for scared kids to—how you say—yell for help."

"A cry for help, son?"

"Dass it, for true, Gabe. A *cry for help*."

"If there was, what a miracle it could be," Gabe said.

"Has to be some easy way, so they don't get caught doin' it by pimps and get beat like I saw on Carrollton."

"A secret signal."

"Dass for true, Gabe."

Gabe rubbed his chin with his hand.

"A quiet shout for help," Gabe said.

"If it's a good one, Gabe, it'll make a loud noise. A signal kids can use to ask for help without gettin' in trouble with no bastard pimp."

"A signal the world will recognize."

"You plenty smart, think of something, Captain. You been in army so long you have to know something that will work."

Gabe stood up from his chair.

"Give me a walk around the block, and I'll come up with a signal by the time I get back."

Peck watched the old man put his newsboy cap on, grab a cane and walk out the door. As the door closed Peck's phone lit up with a call from Millie.

"Hello Millie, love of my life. How you are?"

"Are you in Baton Rouge, Peck?"

"No, your Peck is home, havin' chicory with Gabe."

"Anything exciting happen while you were gone?"

"Nah nah, bébé. What were you doing last night? You doing tests this week?"

"All week, but I think I can come in two weeks. Will you be happy to see me?"

"Oh my, I be so happy. I miss you so much."

"I love you, Peck."

"I love you too, pretty lady. I miss you."

"Peck if I did something stupid, would you still love me?"

"I will love you no matter what, Millie. I do stupid things but loving you ain't one of them. I'll tell Lily Cup you comin' in two weeks. She be happy. She say files piling up."

They ended the call.

At Lily Cup's house in the Garden District, the soft sounds of Johnny Mathis filled a morning kitchen while a tub upstairs slowly filled with warm water and Lily Cup in an apron filled a thermos with cinnamon chicory. Her front doorbell rang and with a dish towel in hand she opened the door. A tall, elegant black man stood there and greeted Lily Cup with a gentle smile.

"You've got some singing voice, big guy," Lily Cup said.

"My *Johnny Hartman*?" Larry asked. "I've been singing Johnny Hartman ever since my voice changed and my daddy played me one of his old records."

"They need a singer like you at Charlie's Blue Note. Come in, big guy."

"Let me take my shoes off," Larry said. "Wading in puddles since 3 a.m.—no let up and I don't want to track."

"I'll get some newspaper to set them on."

Larry stepped in and looked about as if his heart was filled with familiar memories.

"Oh my," Larry said. "It's been a while."

"I see you in court, Larry. It hasn't been that long."

"I mean since I've been in this house."

"Oh?"

"It's just the same. I love this house."

"You've been here? In this house before?"

"You were at Harvard, I think. I remember you were tied up with classes or law exams or something. I was a young Turk and considering my choices, one being a career in the army. Your daddy invited my dad and me to dinner one night to show me options, to help me decide. I'll never forget it. Your daddy was a great man. He inspired me."

"He got me through my law exams," Lily Cup said. "Failed twice, Daddy told me I had to either do it right or think of becoming a plumber."

"Well, that was a quick look at reality, I'd say," Larry said.

"I miss him every day," Lily Cup said.

Lily Cup noticed a shopping bag sitting on the base of the hat and umbrella stand. She looked inside. In it was the black handbag Peck had asked her to get fingerprints lifted from. The bag he said he had taken home. Unbeknownst to her, it was the bag with the fingerprints of the man Peck has since murdered. Her housekeeper found it upstairs, put it in a shopping bag. Lily Cup handed Larry the shopping bag.

"I need to get prints read. My housekeeper must have found it upstairs. Can you get prints read with all you have going on?"

Larry took the shopping bag. He pulled the Ziplock bag from it and looked at the black purse inside.

"The prints should be good," Larry said.

He set the shopping bag next to his shoes.

"Give me a couple days, I'll get answers," Larry said.

"Tub's running, big guy. Go soak. Lazy morning, so no hurry, come down when you're ready and we'll do brunch. I've got reading to catch up on."

"I want to thank you for the hospitality, my friend. You saved me a long drive to Covington and back," Larry said. "I'll go soak my bones. Pouring rain can take a toll on an old man."

"Stop it, Larry. You're so not old."

"You know how to charm a guy, kitten. I'll give you that."

"You're my age, big guy. A very handsome man."

Larry smiled and headed for the stairs.

"If there's an FBI file, I'll have names for the prints," Larry said.

He smiled and started up the stairs in his socks.

32.

GABE CAME IN FROM HIS WALK around the block.

"Story time, my brother," Gabe said.

"Sounds like you been thinkin' good, Captain."

They settled in the living room.

Even more than being a good fisher and good tracker, Peck loved being a good student. He listened to every word and learned like a vacuum cleaner fed his brain. He'd listen to teachers as if they were storytellers.

"We're going to talk signals, son."

"Dass good, Gabe. Thanks."

"International signals."

"Hanh?"

"International, son. That means signals that mean the same thing all over the world."

"Even better, Gabe."

"Early in the twentieth century, Peck, Germany came up with a signal the world embraced."

"That's what we need, how you say, international. Now you're talkin'."

"Every nation used it all the way through the second world war, son."

"What was it Gabe?"

"SOS, son."

"SOS?"

"SAVE OUR SHIP, SOS."

"I don't get it, Gabe."

"Peck, why can't the kids use it now? SOS–SEX O SLAVE?"

"It still means trouble, Gabe?"

"SOS will always mean big trouble son."

"How's it work, Gabe?"

"The sex slave goes into a restroom in the lobby and scratches a big SOS on the toilet stall wall. Maybe even in lipstick on the mirror. A big SOS—and inside the O they write the room number where they just came from or the number of the room they are going to. Imagine Peck—in time word will spread what it means and someone will call for help when they see SOS with the room number in it. It'll mean *Sex Slave in room 402*, or 531, whatever."

"If they're leaving, Gabe. What good would it do?"

"They leave a date. That's it, son. If they leave a date the cops or the hotel can trace the room and date to the person who rented the room and broke the law as a sex trafficker. They probably couldn't arrest him after the fact, but the hotel sure could ban him from future visits."

"I like it, Gabe. I like it a lot."

"It works, doesn't it son? SOS – sex slave, help!"

"Gabe what if they're on a street being slaved or maybe somewhere around people?"

"Then they can use an SOS hand signal. They see a cop or someone who could help them, they hold their hand down at their side, make a fist and open and close three fingers three times in a row. It's Morse code. Three fingers —dot, dot, dot—three fingers—dash, dash, dash—three fingers—dot, dot, dot."

Peck practices the signal.

"SOS, Sex Slave Help!" Peck said. "That'll work sure. Starting today. You're a master, Captain. You think good this time, ol' man."

"An SOS finger scratch, son. A three-finger scratch. A cry for help. Why, every maid will call the hotel manager, every housekeeper, every flight attendant will inform the captain, every decent human being on earth who sees it will know what the signal means and will come to a sex slave's rescue and tell a cop."

Gabe convinced Peck the word would spread like wildfire and soon the world would know the signal and hotels would have a record of who sex trafficked by the room numbers and dates.

Peck went to his room to think how to communicate the signal to Lauren and hotel concierges. SOS with date and room number on bathroom walls, or the three finger, three-time crunch signal cry for help. All of the pedicab drivers Lauren could trust should be taught the signal to teach slaves they came in contact with.

33.

LILY CUP WAS ON HER SOFA reading when she glanced over at Larry's wet shoes on the newspaper by the door. She got up, got two mugs and the thermos and went upstairs and into the master bedroom. She could hear the lieutenant's low bass humming in the tub through the door.

"Feeling refreshed, big guy?" she asked.

"Would you believe I've had a short catnap in this fabulous old tub?" Larry asked. "Sorry if I'm holding up brunch."

"I can't remember a time in that tub when I haven't been snoozing," Lily Cup said. "Thought you'd like some coffee. Might a lady join you?"

"Me in a tub is not a pretty sight— enter at your risk."

Lily Cup opened the bathroom door, stepped in and closed it behind her. She set the mugs and thermos on the table next to the tub.

"Let me show you a trick," Lily Cup said.

She knelt and leaned over the tub and began twisting knobs.

"If you open this drain just a peep—just a tad like this—and then open the hot water to a drip, this baby will keep you all toasty-pruny for a good long soak."

Elbows rested on the tub, Lily Cup took her time checking out Larry's chest, thighs, and golden brown eyes.

"You've still got it, big guy."

"Wonderful thing, aging," Larry mused.

"I've always had a crush on you," Lily Cup said.

"Pushing forty, eyes—first thing to go," Larry said.

Lily Cup grinned and stared at his eyes with her hand rested on his thigh. His eyes smiled and she moved her hand over his thigh to his groin, grabbing his package.

"Oh my," Lily Cup said.

"Oh my, indeed," Larry whispered.

Lily Cup smiled.

"It's been a while," Larry said.

Under the warm bath water Lily Cup stroked his package with fingers, feeling it grow.

Larry reached around Lily Cup's head and gently pulled her for a kiss. It was a passionate kiss, a kiss between two friends from years past who had always known they had something, things in common—a mutual admiration, mutual respect. He rested back and smiled.

"To what do I owe this pleasure?" Larry whispered.

Lily Cup didn't answer but stood, pulled her top and bra off and stuffed them behind a towel rack. She pushed her panties and tights to the floor, stepped out of them and kicked them aside.

"I've been stalking you for years," Lily Cup said.

"I could have you arrested," Larry quipped.

She moved the small table and stepped to the side of the tub nearest him.

"Bring your cuffs, big guy?"

Larry's warm hand reached her inner thigh and slid sensuously up its velvety white, his fingertips reaching, kneading her love island, gently searching for a warmth of its moist fruit, like a delicate French pastry.

"It's been a while for me too," Lily Cup whispered.

Lily Cup stepped in the tub and straddled his waist.

"Here I come, ready or not," she whispered.

"Oh my," she whispered.

"Oh my, indeed," Larry mumbled.

34.

PECK BOOKMARKED HIS COPY of *Of Mice and Men* and texted Lauren.

"Call me when you're not working, frien'."

"I can call now. Want me to?"

Peck pressed her number.

"Hey," Lauren said.

"How you are, bébé?"

"My roommate lent me a skirt and thigh-high socks for Zydeco tonight. Are we still going?"

"Ah *oui*."

"I can't wait. I've been looking at nursing schools in Baton Rouge. That was so much fun last night with you and Elizabeth. Thank you."

"Elizabeth my special frien', bébé, I know her like since I was seventeen, I think. Maybe longer."

"I love how you hold each other. I want to be held like that."

"Zydeco is holdin' hands and two-steppin,' bébé, do they slow Zydeco?"

"There's lots of slow dancing too."

"I hold you good then, dass for true."

"What'd you want to talk about, Peck?"

"Oh, that—my frien' Gabe here come up with a signal sex slaves like Tiffany can use to— how you say— *cry for help* without getting' beat up."

"He did?"

"What we got to figure out is how we can tell pedicab drivers and the concierges, ever'body, what the signal is so they can teach slaves and hope they pass it around."

"I can do that," Lauren said.

"Hanh?"

"I can do that, easy."

"You can?"

"Can I come over? I'll show you how I can do it."

"Okay, sure."

"Where do you live?"

"Garden District."

"Do you have a driveway?"

"Yes."

Peck gave her the address.

"See you soon, Peck."

"Okay, good, bébé. See you soon."

"Peck?"

"Ah *oui*?"

"Can I bring things for tonight and change there?"

"Sure thing."

They ended the call.

As Peck, on his bedroom floor, read more of his *Of Mice and Men* novel, Lily Cup was on her side behind Larry, scratching his back.

"You have a beautiful body," Lily Cup said.

Larry rested a hand on her thigh behind him.

"That was beyond words," Lily Cup whispered.

"The word *speechless* comes to mind," Larry said. "Woman, I don't know where you get your energy."

"It's been no secret, big guy. Tulip had an itching for a scratchin' since high school."

"Tulip?" Larry quipped. "I won't ask."

"I'm Lily Cup and she's Tulip, simple as that."

"How did you get such a curious name? Lily Cup— there has to be a story."

"You've never heard it?"

"I haven't."

Lily Cup leaned on his shoulder.

"I was conceived on a picnic blanket in Chalmette in 1981. Daddy was introducing me into my momma, so to speak, right next to a wooden bowl of potato salad. Momma rolled in passion, her bare butt cheeks crushing a tube of Lily Tulip paper cups they brought for their mint juleps—and a julep isn't a drink you can drink from a bottle. Nine months to the day Daddy wanted to name me Tulip, Momma made him promise he wouldn't. And he didn't. He wrote *Lily Cup* on my birth certificate."

"Your daddy was a fascinating man. I'll never forget him inviting me and my pop over here for dinner. He cooked white fish and okra, and we sat and he gave me career advice, showing me options, offering to open some doors for me. I'll never forget it."

Larry's phone rang in the bathroom.

"I may need to get that," Larry said.

Lily Cup rolled over and got out of bed. She retrieved his phone from the table next to the tub and brought it around to his side of the bed and handed it to him.

"Chris, what'cha got?"

"Did you get some rest, Lieutenant?"

"I'm a new man."

"I have some things to go over, if you can come in."

"Chris, might I bring a lady friend with me?"

"I wouldn't if she has a weak stomach."

"It's Lily Cup Tarleton, Chris."

"Oh, I know her. Sure, bring her along."

"Give us half an hour," Larry said.

The call ended.

35.

GABE RAPPED ON PECK'S bedroom door and opened it slightly.

"You awake Peck? You have a friend here."

"Ah *oui*."

Peck stood up and tossed his book on the bed.

Gabe opened the door and let Lauren in. Peck introduced them as she laid a shopping bag and a laptop on the bed.

"May I get you anything, young lady? Iced tea? Lemonade?" Gabe asked.

"Do you have any water?" Lauren asked.

"Coming up."

"I love this house, Peck. Are you like roommates?"

"Nah-nah—Gabe, he like a father to me, bébé. I'll tell you sometime. You'll like the story, dass for true."

"Want to see my skirt for tonight?"

"Ah *oui*, for sure."

Lauren lifted a black pleated skirt from the bag and held it up. It came halfway down her thighs.

"I'm taller than she is, but we have the same waist. I'll have thigh-high socks on too. You think the skirt is too short on me?"

"Nah-nah, it's perfect, I think. Peck be proud to be dancin' with you, bébé."

Gabe brought in a bottled water and stepped out, pulling the door closed.

Peck demonstrated the SOS "cry for help" signal and how it was developed from an old maritime distress signal known all over the world. He explained the idea of a slave writing SOS with room numbers and dates on the walls of bathroom stalls and mirrors. He explained that it might take time for the world to learn the signal, but it won't take long.

"How can we tell pedicab drivers first, bébé?" Peck asked.

"Watch this," Lauren said.

She squatted on the floor, sat with back to a wall and rested the laptop on her lap. Peck sat on the floor beside her.

"My Millie knows these things too—computers. You know 'em to, I see."

"Pretty much have to," Lauren said. "I take some nursing classes on it and my exams."

On the screen she opened a website where public transport drivers, pedicabs, taxi, horse carts, bus drivers, and even limo drivers in New Orleans can post notices. The messages would stay up a week and be taken down. She used her iPhone to video her hand making the SOS signal. She uploaded that.

"Peck, this is where I tell everybody about the code, the SOS. I tell them to teach it, but be careful, not get caught by a pimp, but they can save lives by teaching it."

"And all those people will see this?" Peck asked.

"Everyone who goes on this site will—well, drivers, that is."

"When, bébé? When will they see it?"

"Some could be reading it right now. It's posted and the site has approved the post and the upload."

Peck put his arms around Lauren, giving her a hug and a kiss on the cheek. She crunched her neck with a shy, happy grin of accomplishment.

"That's a hold, bébé, but tonight I hold you better."

Lauren leaned over and kissed Peck on the cheek.

"That's for last night," Lauren said.

She closed the computer and set it on the floor. She stood and sat on the bed, lifting his book.

"Are you reading this?"

"Ah *oui*. I like John Steinbeck."

She gathered her thoughts, set the book on the bed and reached in her bag and lifted out thigh-high socks.

"Peck, can I ask you something?"

He sat next to her.

"Ah *oui*, anything, bébé. Ax."

"Are we really going to try to save Tiffany? You can tell me the truth. I mean I know we said a lot of things and

Audrey told us a lot of things, but it's dangerous. Are we really going to try to save her?"

Peck touched her chin and pulled her face to his.

"I promise with ever'thing I got, bébé, we goin' to save your frien' Tiffany. I promise you, and dass for true."

Lauren leaned in and kissed him a warm *thank you* kiss.

"Truth?" she whispered.

"Truth," Peck said.

She kissed him again, and picked up two pairs of long socks.

"Which color, Peck? Black or red? To go with the skirt tonight, Zydeco. Black or red?"

"Oh bébé, you pick. I hold you good in anything you wearin'."

As Peck and Lauren conferred about socks and Zydeco and of signals and saving Tiffany, Lily Cup and Lieutenant Larry Gaines, detective, pulled in to park at the New Orleans city morgue. They made their way in and into the refrigerated holding room.

"Counselor Tarleton, so good to see you," Coroner Chris O'Sullivan said.

Not one to be patronized, Lily Cup stopped short.

"Chris, in the fourth grade we crawled under your gramma's back porch to play doctor. I've seen your penis. Don't be Counselor Tarleton-ing me."

"Remember that spider?" Chris asked.

"Spider?" Larry asked. "I don't do spiders."

"There was a wolf spider in the corner staring at us," Chris said.

"I was ten and about to drop dead," Lily Cup said. "I wasn't about to drop my knickers with a spider from Hell staring up at me—I got the hell out of there fast, cutting short my anatomy lesson … with our doctor here."

"So what'cha got for me Chris?" Larry asked.

Chris stepped one by one over to four of the bodies and pulled the covers down to their chests.

"These four were in the dumpster, Lieutenant. All four died by asphyxiation. All four with a constrictor knot in a single strand of 250-pound test fishing line."

"Constrictor, Chris? That knot and the clove hitch are deadly knots, right?"

"Almost impossible to get them undone, Lieutenant. All four were alive when tossed into the dumpster. Their hands and feet weren't tied. Whoever ordered these executions knew these victims would panic trying to get the knot undone and wouldn't waste time trying to climb out. They all choked to death in the dumpster. One of them, number three over there, had the fishing line around his neck sever his jugular. He bled until his heart stopped, but he died of asphyxiation not blood loss. His face was resting on a plastic garbage bag and panic caused him to swallow his own blood."

"Any clues who might have done it?" Larry asked.

"Forensics says this is a professional job, Lieutenant. That's all we know. No prints, no fibers, no footprints. Heavy rain washes sins away, and it was pouring all night. Weapon was three feet of fishing line on each victim. Only possible clues might be the handwriting. Check their foreheads, Lieutenant. XII is carved on their foreheads."

"Forensics have any idea about the meaning of XII, Chris?"

"The Hanged Man," Lily Cup said.

"Come again?" Larry asked.

"Tarot," Lily Cup said. "The Hanged Man card."

Larry looked at Chris.

"As God is my judge, Chris, I've not said a word to this woman about the Hanged Man," Larry said.

"Radio news said he was hanged," Lily Cup said. "They even said it looked Satanic. Only makes sense to a N'Orleans lady the murder was The Hanged Man copycat murder."

"See why I like her so much, Lieutenant?"

"I surely do, Chris. Probably the smartest criminal attorney wearing her knickers in Louisiana."

"Lily Cup?" Chris asked. "Would you defend a child molester, a slave trafficker?"

"Is that a trick question, Chris?"

"Would you?"

"Sure, if they plead guilty."

"See why I like her, Lieutenant?"

"What else you got, Chris?"

Chris pulled the cover down from the hanged man.

"This corpse was dead an hour before his cervical fracture."

"Before his what?" Larry asked.

"Neck," Lily Cup said.

"His neck was broken when they hung him," Chris said.

"Talk to me, Chris," Larry said.

"Lieutenant, my theory is whoever did this found his room, got in, tied twenty strands of fishing line around his neck, threatening to kill him if he didn't show on his website who was coming for sex and to what rooms. Whoever did this would have had someone go into the rooms they watched from a distance in the rain.

"When the girl came out to goes back to her room, my theory is they rushed the room she came out of, walked the guy at gunpoint to the dumpster, cut his forehead with a knife and tossed him in, while yanking a constrictor knot that he didn't know was put around his neck while walking around to the back of the motel. My guess is the girl coming out of the rooms was their signal."

"I think you're close to it on the dumpster, Chris. How about our Christmas ornament here?"

"He was dead before he was tossed. Whoever was in the vehicle started it when he was pushed over the rail, the pusher comes down the stairs, gets into the vehicle and away they all went."

"Pretty efficient, Chris."

"Lieutenant, three guys could have done this whole thing."

"Think about this, Chris," Larry said. "One guy breaks into Christmas ornament's room, tortures him with fishing line and gets a heads up on at least four of the rooms the pregnant girl was going to service. There could have been more rooms, but he's a pro, he's on a clock. He strangles him, ties him up all fancy-like, with rope and then he goes to his vehicle and waits. One by one he takes a john to the dumpster at gunpoint, cuts him, makes the guy climb in on his own or get shot, and he pulls the constrictor then and cuts the line. He goes back to his vehicle and waits for number two, then number three, then number four."

"And after number four is in the dumpster," Lily Cup said, "he goes up, pushes the guy over, gets in his vehicle and drives away in the rain."

"One-man job, maybe. Sonofabitch," Larry said.

"Maybe a plate, Lieutenant? A video somewhere?" Chris asked.

"No cameras in Gert Town, Chris. They get stolen as fast as they put them up."

Chris walked to the sixth table, pulled the cover sheet down to the chest of the corpse. Lily Cup saw the large bright red tattoo of the dollar sign on the neck. She stepped closer.

"This one's a pimp, right?" Lily Cup asked.

"Big time. Lily Cup, you have a feel for investigative work," Larry said.

Lily Cup examined closer.

"Chris, are his ears pierced?"

"They are. Forensics have the diamond studs."

"Come up with anything on barcodes?" Larry asked.

"Barcodes?" Lily Cup asked.

"You're not going to believe it, Lieutenant. Help me turn him."

They rolled the body of the pimp onto its side.

"Lieutenant, look how each of these barcodes are spaced apart and toward the side of his butt cheek?"

"I can see that," Larry said.

"Notice anything peculiar, Lieutenant?"

"Talk to me, Chris."

"They're all backward. They're reversed."

"And …?"

"Each of these barcodes has a name connected to a bank account. These barcodes are deposit codes for one of the sex slaves. This is a bookkeeping system, Lieutenant."

"Why are they reversed, Chris— backward?"

"Two reasons, Lieutenant. First is he drops his pants, scans a barcode in a mirror and deposits the john's payment for sex, pulls his pants up and has no evidence on him."

"And the second?" Larry asked.

"With the barcodes reversed, Lieutenant, they can't be read by electrical barcode scanners or readers he walks by. Least that's what forensics thinks."

"Sonofabitch," Larry said.

"Chris?" Lily Cup asked. "So, like let's say one of the slaves is a Tiffany, are you saying there's a barcode on his ass for Tiffany?"

"Funny you should pick that name. Just so happens one of these is titled Tiffany," Chris said.

Lily Cup was mesmerized—her lips tensed; her eyes glared at the barcodes on the pimp's buttocks. She shook her head awake.

"What would happen if, like, this Tiffany ran away or died or something?" Lily Cup asked.

"They name another girl Tiffany and use the same barcode," Larry said.

"Lily Cup, I've seen barcodes on girl's necks and boy's wrists. Some slaves branded like cattle. Their barcodes tell how much per hour, what they'll do," Chris said. "That way, if they get caught they get arrested and charged with prostitution and it doesn't trail back to a pimp."

Larry thanked Chris for the good work, told him his team was going into an evidence meeting in the morning and they might ask him to join. He and Lily Cup walked out of the room, through the corridor and out to the parking area. Lily Cup hesitated.

"Larry …?" Lily Cup started.

"What'cha need, kitten?"

"You know the black bag I gave you? For prints?"

"It's in my trunk," Larry said.

"My guess is that pimp guy's prints are on that bag."

"Talk to me," Larry said.

"I can't. Larry you're going to have to trust me on this one."

"Withholding evidence …?" Larry started.

"Forget you, Larry. It's client privilege then."

"Don't get sore, I wasn't—"

"I asked you to trust me, and you go off on me."

"I apologize, all my heart. I'll even give you the bag back. Take it, I'll pop the trunk."

"Good, I'll return it."

Larry drove Lily Cup home.

"We're dancing tonight, unless you have better offers," Larry said.

"You're not mad at me?"

Larry ignored her. "You really see Chris's penis?"

Lily Cup grinned.

"Larry, that was a dream—you and me."

"I'll drop you home, cross Ponchartrain to Covington, do what has to be done, take a nap, and pick you up tonight. We'll dance jazz and see what else comes up."

Lily Cup grinned.

"You think The Hanged Man murders were done by one man, Larry?"

"Looking at the timing of deaths, no doubt in my mind. The murderer got what he needed from the Christmas ornament and strangled him. Took his time and tied him, probably using a Tarot card for instructions. Then he picked off the johns one by one, promising them if they crawled into the dumpster on their own as punishment, he wouldn't shoot them. Not telling them he had already slipped fishing line over their head and around their neck in the rain."

"Jesus," Lily Cup said.

"We dance tonight?" Larry asked.

"Larry, let me ask you something. Prostitution has been around a long time."

"Oldest profession in the world."

"Some women depend on it. How would you know if it's for real a gal just trying to make a living or a sex slave?" Lily Cup asked.

"Well, it's illegal— but that's not your question. My best guess is she'll answer her own phone if she's on her own and her john would put the money in her hand."

"See you tonight. Get a good nap, big guy."

36.

HEARING A KNOCK, Gabe went to the side door. It was Damas, the Southern Louisiana researcher for author Simon Dermott.

"Gabe, I see a pedicab in your driveway. You have company? Am I interrupting anything?" Damas asked.

"Come in, my brother. Come in."

Gabe brought Damas into the living room and invited him to sit as he took a bowtie from the mantle and began pulling it under his shirt collar.

"I was passing by and thought I'd ask to see if you were maybe going to Charlie's tonight and may I join you."

"Always, my brother. The only incentive this ol' soul needs to go to Charlie's for jazz and dancing is a ride and the promise of a Chivas."

As they talked, Peck came out from his bedroom and joined them. He was buttoning a black shirt Elizabeth had given him in Baton Rouge.

"Hi Peck, how's it going?" Damas asked.

"Ever'thing good by me, bébé. Where you at?"

"I'm going to Charlie's with Gabe to enjoy some jazz you told me about and maybe chat Creole when he's not dancing," Damas said. "Will you be joining us?"

"Nah-nah, tonight frien' I Zydeco. Washboard, jingle jangle, you know."

Lauren came into the room. Gabe introduced her to Damas.

"Lady, you look like you just stepped from a Saks window, you look dashing," Gabe said.

"I do?" Lauren asked with a shy smile. "You don't think it's too short?"

"Honey, God gifted you legs, your pedicab keeps them fantastic. That outfit is perfect," Gabe said.

They spoke of Zydeco and of Mulate's, and of maybe meeting up later at Charlie's Blue Note. Damas told Peck what Simon Dermott, the writer, told him about where the movie producer from the Hamptons' second home was in the Garden District. He mentioned the street and number 3054, and he spoke about having spent a few hours with Leah Chase in her kitchen at Dookie Chase, talking about music in the Jim Crow days, how the city had grown and matured and how you never put hot sauce in her gumbo. It was an insult to a chef. He told Gabe about Simon's latest research on trafficking and his surprise in learning that women were a big percentage of the sex traffickers, and family members, lovers, friends or marriage partners were a large percentage, locking their victims into the lifestyle of selling sex by intimidation and threats of abandonment.

Peck found a spot to park and they got out.

"Peck, you have Millie. She sounds sweet, but could we maybe hold hands walking into Mulate's?"

Peck takes her hand.

"You know my Millie, bébé?"

"No, I heard her talking with Elizabeth—in Baton Rouge. She sounded nice."

"She so nice, my Millie. She'll be here in two weeks. You'll meet her then, bébé."

They got a table against a wall and without sitting down, Peck took Lauren by the hand onto the dance floor.

"I'm goin' to watch your feet so good, bébé—teach me good, now."

A high-pitched, mournful sound of an accordion dominated the echoes off the walls, columns, vintage metal signs and the pictures decorating walls. A tinny washboard strapped to a player's chest—fingers in sewing thimbles scratched a rhythm on the ripples only a fool could miss and a background jingle-jangle of hollow cowbell tapped with a stick. Most lyrics were just shout-outs of beer brands or liquor brands. Peck and Lauren held hands with clenched fingers. They'd pull close and push away, ankles turned in and turned out like they were sanding the floor with the soles of their feet. Lauren's skirt danced with turns and Peck rolled his head with closed eyes, as if the sounds reminded him of the wood sawmills he grew up listening to from the blade shed behind his cot. Zydeco was a reminder of a routine in life, that life was a monotony if we didn't dance, and if we twisted our feet in and out and girls let their hips twist and turned so their skirts showed some pretty leg, that was a good thing, and the Cajun food was so good it was worth a rest.

Peck held her hand and led her to the table. He picked up a napkin and wiped his brow.

"You want you some alligator bites, bébé, or maybe some fried calamari or some crawfish pie?"

"Can I have crawfish pie? A Bud Lite will do me," Lauren said. "I have money."

Peck memorized what to order.

"How'd I do, bébé? I stompin' on you?" Peck asked.

"That was so much fun. You did really good. Thank you for bringing me, Peck. Your Millie is lucky."

"You say you talked with my Millie, bébé?"

"I didn't, Elizabeth did—I just overheard."

"I wonder why Elizabeth talk to my Millie."

"I don't know. Millie called—oh wait, that's right— Millie called your phone and you were gone to the store or something and you forgot your phone."

"Ah *oui*."

"Millie was worried or something, and Elizabeth told her not to worry, that you had a secret phone number to call if you ever saw anyone getting slaved," Lauren said.

"Elizabeth give her the number, bébé? How—?"

"No. Elizabeth didn't give her any number—I didn't tell her the number—she just told Millie there was a number and not to worry, that you were safe."

"Ah—okay then."

"I would never tell the number to anyone you didn't want me to tell."

"How did Elizabeth know about a number, bébé?"

"She didn't know the number. You left a *The Hanged Man* card on your phone. Elizabeth asked me why you wanted a Tarot reading, and if you were doing anything dangerous. I told her not to worry. There was a number you could call, but I never told her the number."

"Okay," Peck said. "Keep the number secret outside of—how you say—drivers and concierges."

"Peck?"

"Hanh?"

"Can we go to your place?"

"When?"

"Now? Can we?"

"We done dancin' bébé?"

"Can we?"

"You okay, bébé?"

"I want to go somewhere and just talk. I want to hold hands, feel normal. Can we?"

"Ah *oui*, we'll go to our place. Gabe is dancin'. We'll talk plenty good."

Lauren stood up.

"Thank you, Peck."

As Peck and Lauren held hands and walked on Julia Street to find his pickup and go to the shotgun, Gabe and Sasha danced to Joe Williams's sounds at Charlie's.

"Now she is gone—" Gabe sang into Sasha's ear as his hips paused, turned to the sounds of the velvety saxophone— vaaaa vaaaa voooooom—his hips pushed and swung tuned to a rhythm. Sasha's arm around his neck, her eyes closed— he sang as they glided the floor.

"All my eyes could weep but I've gotta keep them dry—'cause the man ain't supposed to cry."

The song ended with the band beginning its break, clapping their hands for their favorite dance partners, brother Gabe and his dance mate Sasha in her Givenchy strapless. Gabe led her to the table where Lily Cup, Larry Gaines, and Damas were discussing body bags destroying DNA evidence if the body is wet.

"Will you three turn the business of death off awhile and just enjoy the sounds of living?" Gabe asked. "There are more important issues to discuss at this table."

"Sasha," Larry started, "excuse my stares—I couldn't take my eyes off your moves with a brother to an inimitable champion of sound, brother Joe Williams. You are divine."

"Never ever had a better dance partner than this lug here—and thank you for the nice words," Sasha said.

"What could be more important at this table, Gabe?" Lily Cup asked. "We're the murder capital of the—"

"Well for one, I'm out of Chivas. For two, I haven't seen you take my beautiful brother onto that floor, and you've been here no telling how long, jawing murders and bodies." Gabe guffawed.

Damas stood.

"That settles it," Damas said. He grinned. "The next two rounds are on me. Give me a few to fight the crowd. I shall return."

He walked away.

"He's an interesting young man, that Damas," Gabe said to Larry. "Just imagine—three brothers at a table in New Orleans, three brothers sitting with two beautiful piano-ivory white ladies—two of the most successful ladies in the state, as it was always meant to be in the eyes of God, but never witnessed in a lifetime by my dear momma or my good father. The mere thought or suggestion of such a thing could have cost them their lives."

"Now who's getting maudlin?" Sasha asked.

Lily Cup teased, "I love chocolate."

"Girlfriend," Sasha started, "so what's taking so long?"

"What's taking so long?" Lily Cup asked.

"You two—hooking up—you and our basketball star sweetheart you're sitting next to?"

Lily Cup stood and took Larry's hand as he stood, towering beside her.

"Who says we haven't?" Lily Cup asked.

She and Larry embraced and danced into a blues number. Lily Cup winked at Sasha.

As Larry and Lily Cup melted together, she hummed into his chest, his Johnny Hartman groans casted a spell that blended them as the same minds on a mountaintop, watching the stars.

In the Garden District, Peck and Lauren turned the kitchen lights on and stepped into his bedroom.

"Where you want to talk, bébé? Anyplace be good?"

Lauren unbuttoned her skirt and dropped it to the floor.

"Do you have a candle, Peck?"

"I think we do. Let me look."

As Peck went into the kitchen, Lauren took her top and bra off, pulled a T-shirt on and lay on the bed in her thigh-high socks, panties and T-shirt, holding Peck's John Steinbeck novel she had picked off the desk, *The Grapes of Wrath*. Peck came in and closed the door behind him.

"I found one, bébé. It's a big, fat one. Gabe always say fat candles safer because they don't tip over. Where you want it?"

"How about on the desk?"

"Okay."

Peck set the candle on his desk. He turned the room light off and lit it. He leaned in, staring at it before turning toward the bed.

"Is this a good book?" Lauren asked.

"Oh, that is so good a book, bébé. So good."

Peck unbuttoned his shirt, took it off and hung it.

"Where you from, bébé? I forgot."

"Oklahoma. Why?"

Peck dropped his jeans to the floor, stepped out and kicked them into the closet. In briefs and no top, he circled the bed and sat down.

"Bébé, that book starts in Oklahoma in depression time. That's when the country was poorer than an alley cat and people starved. It was so sad with how they starved. The girl's baby died. Brand new baby too."

"That's so sad. Does it have a happy ending at least?"

"That momma, bébé?"

"The one whose baby died?"

"Dass it … Well they come to this rusty old railroad car that was not hitched on a rail like it was in a field or something just rusting out, but there was a man inside it laying in the corner. He was dying, bébé, dass for true."

Lauren raised up on her elbow and leaned toward Peck listening to the story.

"Why was the man dying?"

"He was starved almost to death. I think maybe like he ain't had food in longest time, bébé."

"Did he die?"

"Know what she done, that girl? That new momma whose baby died? Know what she done?"

"Tell me."

"She got on her knees next to the man. He couldn't move he was so starved, so she helped him and she opened her shirt and put a tit in his mouth and told him to go ahead and take her baby's milk, that God say for her to do that. John Steinbeck don't say, bébé, but I think her baby milk saved that man's life maybe."

In the candle glow, Peck could see tears forming in Lauren's eyes. He didn't interrupt her imagination, but sat there still, satisfied that he had delivered Steinbeck's message with integrity. With tears dripping down her cheeks, Lauren rested back on a pillow. Her right hand reached for Peck's hand and gripped his thumb. Her left thumb she lifted to her mouth and suckled. It comforted her. Peck made little notice, remembering how traumatized she was the night tattoo dollar sign put a gun in her face and hit Tiffany. Lauren looked up at Peck. She pulled the thumb from her mouth.

"That's a beautiful story. Thank you."

She put the thumb back in her mouth.

"I like John Steinbeck, dass for true, he told good stories."

"Do I look silly, sucking my thumb?"

"Nah-nah, not ever, bébé. Peck here stared at the full moon and talked to it, dass for true."

"My boyfriend got me smoking, and I wanted to quit, and it was so hard a doctor in nursing school told me to suck my thumb. So I do."

"Ah *oui*. Smart."

"That was a beautiful story."

"Ah *oui*."

"Kiss me, Peck?"

37.

DAMAS POLITELY EXCUSED HIMSELF and left Charlie's for home at eleven. It was midnight when Larry and Gabe were spooning into their bowls of red beans and rice that had been on the table for two hours. Sasha and Lily Cup visited the rest room. The band was a few minutes into their break when Larry's phone signaled.

"Talk to me," Larry said.

"You in Covington or in town, Larry?"

"Chief?"

"In person."

"I'm on Frenchman Street, Chief. What's up?"

"Four bodies need your attention, Lieutenant."

"I'm not finished with my red beans."

"Get this, Larry. Four bodies already in body bags."

"So, Chris has been there, Chief?"

"That's just the point, Larry. Nobody's been here."

"What!?"

"I'm standing on the top step of the courthouse in my tuxedo and Mariam's waiting for me in the car. We were at a charity thing, pulled out of parking across the street— I made an illegal U-turn—I'm the fucking police chief for Christ's sake! Made it at Tulane and Broad when Miriam screamed, telling me she saw dead bodies on the top steps of the criminal court—2700 Tulane and Broad. I'm looking at four body bags with dead bodies in them."

"Does Chris even know, Chief?"

"I called him before I called you. He asked me to unzip one of the bags to see a face."

"And—?"

"Knife carving on the forehead."

"Here we go, again."

"Means something to you, I'm guessing?"

"You'll hear tomorrow, Chief. Evidence meeting."

"Chris is on his way— a patrol car just pulled up. I'm taking Miriam home. They'll watch over this until you get here. Chris already called forensics."

"Say hi to Miriam, Chief. I'm on my way."

Lily Cup and Sasha sat down.

"What happened, my brother?" Gabe asked.

"Bodies at Tulane and Broad," Larry said.

"Let's go," Lily Cup said, starting to get up.

"Not this time, kitten. Can you catch a ride with Sasha?"

"But why?"

"I'll call you in the morning."

"What aren't you telling me, Larry?" Lily Cup asked.

"Carving on foreheads," Larry whispered.

"Oh?"

Larry stood to leave.

"One?" Lily Cup asked.

Larry held up four fingers. He turned about and left the table and Charlie's. Lily Cup scooted around in her chair and pushed Peck's contact on her iPhone. She let it ring.

"He's not answering," she whispered. "Peck, where are you?"

She called again, got his answer message.

"Peck, where are you? Answer your fucking phone. Peck?"

She hung up. She thought for a moment and pushed the button again.

"Peck, my office tomorrow at nine a.m. Be there. We need to talk."

She started to hang up when a thought jogged her.

"I got the bag you wanted to get the prints read. I know who the prints belong to. I'll give it to you in the morning."

She clicked it off and set it on the table. She thought for a minute and picked it up again and texted Peck.

"BE AT MY OFFICE AT 9 AM!!!!!"

She set the phone down again.

This time Sasha picked Lily Cup's phone off the table and held it.

"Will you calm down, girlfriend?" Sasha asked.

"Sorry."

"What's going on?"

"I think Peck's in trouble," Lily Cup said.

"What kind of trouble?" Sasha asked.

"Big trouble. Serious fucking trouble."

Gabe pushed his bowl away. He neatly folded and set his napkin on top of the bowl.

"This the same young man who found a mother he hadn't seen since he was nine?"

"What does that have—?" Lily Cup started.

"This is the same young man who saved my life? The same young man who taught himself to read—got himself into Tulane?"

"Gabe, you two are peas in a pod, I know you. And you know all about the sex slave—the girl who got beat on Carrollton. So don't bullshit me, Gabe, you know what Peck's been up to. He tells you everything."

"I don't know—"

"Well, he's dead!" Lily Cup shouts.

"Who's dead?"

"The pimp Peck saw beating up that girl!"

"How?"

"Blow to the head! Sound familiar?"

Lily Cup broke into tears.

Gabe slammed his hands on the table.

Lily Cup and Sasha startled.

"I know all I have to know!" Gabe shouted.

He leaned in and lowered his voice.

"This young man has more gumption, more integrity, more drive than any man of any color I have ever met in my lifetime. Now I suggest we all go home, get a good night's rest, and Lily Cup, I am certain your friend and mine will be in your offices in the morning just as you requested. I'm not going to give it another minute of thought."

Without a word spoken Sasha, Lily Cup and Gabe stood up, and started out of Charlie's—Gabe waved at his sax man friend, Sasha blew a kiss over to Charlie.

"Lily Cup," Sasha said. "Tonight, you're sleeping with me, honey. We need hugs."

As Gabe and Lily Cup got in Sasha's Bentley, Lieutenant Larry Gaines was climbing the criminal courthouse building steps, where two uniformed officers and one forensic woman were looking around with flashlights. There were no bodies there.

"Has Chris taken them to the morgue?" Larry asked.

"Lieutenant, Coroner O'Sullivan has taken them to the hospital."

"What!?"

"They were alive, Lieutenant. All four."

Larry bounced down the steps, got in his car and called Chris.

"Go home, get some sleep, Lieutenant. I'm at the University Medical Center with a team of doctors."

"Talk to me, Chris."

"Four men, we have their wallets, their IDs. We know everything about them. One's from Dallas. One's from Charleston. One's from Detroit. One's from Tulsa. All four were drugged on Ketamine."

"Ketamine?"

"It's a liquid you can slip into a drink, Lieutenant. They use it to sedate kids at ER centers when they have to give stitches. These four are in a temporary coma."

"And not dead? And not attempted murders, Chris?"

"Not dead, but you're the detective about attempted murder issues, Lieutenant."

"Why the body bags, Chris?"

"Their foreheads are carved, Lieutenant. We have a 507. We have a 1123, we have a 919 and we have a 740. Other than that, we have nothing."

"Who's with you, Chris?"

"Sergeant Landry, sir."

"Hand him your phone."

"Hello, this is Landry."

"Sergeant, I want guards on these four men all night and when they wake up I want them detained."

"Sir, I don't think we can hold them. They're victims, they really haven't done anything—"

"If we need to, I want them charged with littering, drunk in public, drug influenced, loitering. God dammit Landry, stack it up, but have them at the station in the morning. Call me when they're awake, and I'll even come there."

"Yes, sir. I'll call you first thing they wake up."

"Good."

"Sir, what if they give me an argument or want to call their lawyers?"

"Tell them you know a bastard lieutenant who's thinking of slapping them with suspicions of sex trafficking, best not to piss him off."

"Got it, Lieutenant."

As Larry drove the Lake Ponchartrain causeway home to Covington, Gabe was dropped off by Sasha. In the house Gabe removed his bowtie and tossed it onto the mantle. He pushed Peck's bedroom door open. The candle flickered and Peck and the girl, Lauren, were nestled asleep. Lauren's head on his shoulder with his arm around her as if he was comforting her. Her knee rested on his thigh.

"Peck?" Gabe whispered.

"Hanh?" Peck muffled in whisper.

"Lily Cup needs you in her office at nine a.m., son."

"Okay, thanks."

"Try not to be late, son."

"Wake me. Okay, Gabe?"

Gabe pulled the door closed and went to bed.

38.

PECK WALKED INTO LILY CUP'S OFFICE—
she was sitting in her chair in a cross-legged squat, mug in
hand. She tossed a magazine aside and looked up at him.

"Thanks for coming, Peck."

She pointed at the thermos and mug on the desk.

"How you are, cher?"

"Pull the door."

Peck pulled the door closed.

"Turn your phone off and have a seat."

Peck obliged.

Lily Cup turned her phone off and dropped it on the
cushion between her legs.

"The pimp you watched from the window hitting that
girl is dead, Peck. I saw his body. He's dead."

"Cher, I thought we only talkin' about slavin' things
at your house, never here?"

"Rules have changed, Peck. At my house we were
trying to help a young girl. This Tiffany thing is taking on a
life of its own, and you're holding things in—not being
honest. It's here in this office when somebody needs an
attorney. Today I'm your attorney. You may need one."

"Hanh?"

"I don't want you to say a word, Peck. Not one word,
just sit and listen."

"Okay."

"You're one of my best friends. I know what you had
to go through in life since you were a little boy and this is
going to be hard for me. I've done a lot of thinking and I'm
just going to come out with it. Don't interrupt."

Peck sits back.

"The day you gave me the black bag to get prints read
you told me you saw the girl Tiffany get in a car and have
sex in an alley somewhere. The first night you stayed at my
place, we were drinking heavily. I remember our getting
naked downstairs and you carrying me upstairs and we got

into bed. I don't remember much after that, but I remember waking up the next morning and going downstairs while you were still in bed. Downstairs I picked my clothes up off the floor and put them on the chair. Then I looked. Your clothes weren't on the floor where you left them the night before. Your clothes were gone. That was the morning Larry told me a man in a Porsche was clubbed to death. He said it happened at one a.m. He said it happened in an alley. Is it coincidence, me not remembering midnight or one a.m. and your clothes not being on the dining room floor where you dropped them the night before? Was it coincidence you seeing Tiffany in a car in an alley? That's what you told me. Was it a coincidence a man in a Porsche being killed in an alley?"

Peck was as stoic as a cold tracker in the darkest and deepest bayou swamps where the slightest reflection off an eye could be seen by a predator.

"One night you called me from Charlie's to tell me you were on your way. Peck, I was cooking that night and when you called, I put the cooking timer on. You didn't get there for seventy minutes—should have been seventeen minutes—and you were soaking wet. That night the tattoo pimp was killed by a blow to the head."

Peck was motionless.

"Here's another. I haven't figured this one out yet, but when you were somewhere between New Orleans and Baton Rouge five men were murdered with fishing line, black fishing line. I called your phone and it said you were driving. Larry thinks one man murdered all five. You know what's sad, Peck? I'm trying to see how you might have done those murders. That's how sad this whole mess is. It's killing me."

"I was in Baton Rouge, cher. Gabe showed me about that in the newspaper after I come back, next morning."

"Last night four bodies were left at Tulane and Broad on the criminal court steps. Where were you last night, Peck?"

"I—"

"Don't talk. That was rhetorical," Lily Cup said.

"What you want Peck to do, cher? I can't talk, I just sit here?"

There was a tap on the door. Peck stood and opened it. It was Larry. Larry gave a morning wave.

"Hi," Lily Cup said. "You disappeared last night. You okay?"

"Making progress," Larry said. "Still under wraps, can't discuss it yet."

"Larry?" Peck asked. "Can I see you outside?"

"Sure, let's go."

Peck looked at Lily Cup. Lily Cup looked back.

"Peck, think about your life— where you've been, where you are—where you want to go. Just think about it," Lily Cup said.

"I think it good, cher. I promise."

Larry told Lily Cup he'd be back and he and Peck went through the offices and rode the elevator down. They stepped out of the building when Peck started his pickup from a distance.

"What's on your mind, Peck?"

"I need you to come someplace, Larry."

"Where?"

"Get in my pickup and don't ax, but listen good."

Larry climbed in the pickup and Peck pulled from the curb. He drove to the Saint Louis Basilica parking area.

"Come in with me, Larry. Listen good, but be quiet."

Peck took him into the hallowed basilica where he genuflected, stepped to a confessional with a green light indicating a priest was available and would be forthcoming. Peck pulled the door open and held a curtain to the side. He placed his index finger over his mouth, motioning for Larry to get in the confessional and to stand out of sight against the velvet curtain and witness his confession. Larry paused in reluctance— Peck pulled on his arm insistently. Larry stood inside, next to the curtain. Peck knelt in the dark cubicle and waited. The panel door slid open to a screen.

"Bless me Father, for I have sinned. It has been First Friday when I go see Mamma since my last confession."

"It's good to hear your voice, Boudreaux."

"Father McBride, can I tell you a story before I tell my sins?"

"Yes, my son, tell your story. Take your time."

"Father McBride, my *mémé* (grandma) is in an insane asylum up bayou in Acadiana. *Mémé* is in that place because when she was pregnant with Mamma, she lived in—how you say—Bayou Chene, up bayou. Father McBride, Bayou Chene got swallowed with the Mississippi River … whole town, Father, buried in the silt or somethin', but mémé got out when she saw her whole family drowned and dead—ever'body, Father. Mémé walked all the way to Mandeville and Lake Ponchartrain pregnant. It was cold and rainy, Father, and when she looked up she saw an airplane explode and fall from the moon into Lake Ponchartrain and sink, killin' ever'body. That put my mémé in the insane place, Father, her watching a little girl's red coat and baby doll floating on the lake with dead bodies floating too. My mamma was born in that insane asylum, Father McBride."

"My son, that was tragic—" Father McBride started.

"There's more, Father, I promise a good confession."

Peck told of being a slave when he was five to nine years old, of being chained under a porch by gator man and having to carry bait shrimp buckets until his hands bled and of being pulled behind a boat, his mouth taped so he couldn't scream, to attract alligators for bounty—only being pulled into the boat at the last minute. He told of how a man fathered him by raping his mother and other women in the insane asylum when she was visiting her mamma, his mémé. Of how that same man threatened to kill Dr. Pontelbon with his knife when Dr. Pontelbon discovered that the man raped those ladies, his mamma too. He told how Dr. Pontelbon shot the man with a shotgun, fearing his knife and the man died and floated on the lake. He told how Dr. Pontelbon went right to the sheriff and told him what happened and how that sheriff sent him home and never said another word about it.

"Father McBride. Never a word."

"My son."

"This is my confession, Father McBride: I saw a pimp with a red dollar sign tattooed on his neck. I saw him beat up a girl and hold a gun to her ear and he took her away to sell for sex. Father McBride that girl is Tiffany, and she is twelve years old."

"Oh, my God," Father McBride whispered.

"Father McBride, I conked that pimp. I conked him dead, dass for true."

"Son—"

"Father McBride, I saw a man put Tiffany in a car, she's twelve—he took her in a car and sexed her. I conked him, Father. I conked him too, dass for true."

"My son—Boudreaux, only if you are truly sorry, can I give you Absolution, but I know you, my son, you're a sensitive man. You're a good man."

"Thanks, Father McBride."

"Boudreaux, are you considering telling your story to the police?"

Larry stepped out from the confessional and stood nearby, waiting for Peck.

"I promise, Father McBride."

"For your Penance I want you to say ten rosaries."

"Thanks, Father."

"Go in peace, my son. Please be careful, Boudreaux."

Peck stepped out of the confessional. He and Larry walked to the church's front door and out onto the top stone step. Larry turned, facing Peck. He looked into his eyes. He looked up at the colors of the painted windows, of the stories they told. He looked at the magnificence of church architecture. He looked back at Peck.

"For more than a year I've been hearing from my friend, brother Gabe, and Lily Cup too, of how genuine you are, Peck. You're a good man, an example for others."

"Thanks, Larry."

"I know you help Lily Cup do investigative work."

"Yes, sir."

"I'd consider you for some investigative work ..."

Peck smiled.

"But as to saving this Tiffany business, it's official, you've retired."

"Is that a metaphor, Larry?"

"That's a metaphor, Peck."

"Ah *oui*."

"Is she still in New Orleans?"

"Ah *oui*."

Larry turned his back on Peck, looked up at the sky and turned back around.

"Peck?"

"Yes, sir?"

"I'm going to tell you like it is …"

"Yes, sir."

"I'll close my files on the Porsche guy and the pimp. I'll let it lie, pass them as mob hits—something."

Peck was silent.

"But if you made any mistakes, any mistakes at all."

Larry touched Peck's chest with a pointed finger.

"If forensics find anything that traces back to you, there's no way I can protect you. Understand?"

"I understand."

"Any mistakes—they'll find them."

"I understand."

"Nothing I can do then—if that happens."

"I understand."

"Peck, I listened to your story in there."

"Thanks, Larry."

"It's time to let your past go. You have your mamma. You have your friends. You have to try letting the past go."

"Dass for true. I will, I promise."

Larry shook Peck's hand.

"Do you know where she is?"

"Hanh?"

"That girl, Tiffany?"

"Ah *oui*. She's in Storyville."

"Do we understand each other, Peck? The Tiffany thing on your own, is over."

"Yes, sir."

Larry hugged Peck like a brother.

"Do you know where in Storyville?"

"Ah *oui*."

Peck gave Larry the street address he memorized the night he followed the Mercedes.

"Let's go find her," Larry said.

"For true?" Peck asked.

"Take me to my car, Peck. Hurry."

39.

WHILE PECK RACED through New Orleans, Larry made calls.

"Carol?"

"Yes Lieutenant?"

"Find a judge. I need a search warrant—I need it in minutes."

Larry gave Carol the street address.

"They'll need probable cause, Lieutenant."

"How about two homicides, suspected multiple kidnappings, human trafficking as probable causes, Carol— I have a witness connecting it all together—we're about to make our presence known, Creole style."

"Give me a few, sir," Carol said.

Peck parked behind Larry's car.

"Stay put," Larry said.

He got out of the pickup, went to his car and popped the trunk. He lifted out two vests. He brought one to Peck.

"Put this on, Peck."

"Okay."

Peck took it, put it on and buckled it.

"I'm not deputizing you, and you'll have no police powers, but I am calling on you as a good citizen to aid in the execution of a warrant. Will you assist us?"

"Aye-yi-yi, yes— dass for true."

"Lock this up and jump in my car."

Lights flashed on five police cars as they assumed positions and blocked intersections and exits to a three-story structure in Storyville. The ground floor was vacant and boarded up retail space. On the second and third floors were large dormitory rooms. In the dormitories were two boys under eighteen and fourteen girls from fourteen years of age to twenty-five. Two adult attendants were read their rights, handcuffed and taken to a squad car. Cautious as to not being trapped with legal manipulations, Larry leaned in and whispered in Peck's ear. Peck nodded, stood back, and as a private citizen shouted:

"Raise your hand if you're a sex slave."

Every arm went up.

"How many aren't here?" Peck asked.

"We don't work until later," came a voice.

"Jewel and Tiffany aren't here," a girl said.

"Peter isn't here," a boy shouted.

Larry stepped over by the one who shouted Jewel and Tiffany. He gestured for a lady detective to join him.

"Tell us about Jewel and Tiffany, sweetheart," the lady detective said.

"An old guy buys Tiffany a lot. She hates him. He got Jewel and Tiffany today for something. I don't know. A party or something."

"He's a movie star," a voice shouted.

Peck jolted.

"I know where they are," Peck said.

"Detective, secure the premises," Larry said.

"Warrant, Lieutenant?" the lady detective asked.

"Exigency circumstances, Detective—no time.

"Yes sir."

"I want officers stationed inside at every door. Arrest anyone who comes in under suspicion of human trafficking."

"Yes, Lieutenant."

Larry turned, looked in the empty eyes of sixteen frightened children sitting on the floor with nothing but lost hopes in their hearts.

"Who's hungry?" Larry asked.

Every arm went up.

"Who's up for Popeye's?"

Every arm went up.

"Detective," Larry started. "Take every one of these good kids into protective custody—get them out of here and over to Popeye's for a treat. Get them anything they want."

"Yes sir," the lady detective said.

Larry looked down at the smiles, the hope in eyes.

"Get anything you want, but make sure you get their red beans and rice too, okay? High protein and you're going to need your energy for school."

Larry turned to the lady detective.

"Call DCFS, have them standing by for a special delivery. Let's free these good citizens—get them processed and into counseling with all the help they'll need as soon as possible. No red tape."

Larry pulled the lady detective aside. He handed her a personal VISA card.

"Popeye's is on me, Detective."

"We'll all chip in, Lieutenant," the lady detective said.

"Some of the kids will be drug dependent, Detective. Check the premises for a drug room, paraphernalia, and have a medical aid standby."

"Yes sir."

"The boys, especially. That's how they keep them from running. They hook them."

Larry turned to Sergeant Downs.

"I need backup, Downs— I need it now. Follow us."

Larry waved to the kids and headed to the stairs with Peck and Officer Downs, following him out to the car. As they climbed in, Peck told Larry the street they were headed to.

"It's 3054, Larry."

"Copy that," Larry said.

"Do you need a warrant, Larry?"

"You need a warrant to enter, Peck. You don't need a warrant to knock on a door."

"Ahh. That exigency thing?"

"You remember *exigency*, Peck?"

"I looked it up when'd you said it."

"You are definitely something, my brother."

They pulled onto the street in the Garden District. It was over grown with trees and lined with wrought iron fences with gates. To Peck each mansion seemed bigger than the last. Cars lined both sides of the street, leaving little space. In front of 3054 Larry pulled to a stop. He had no choice but to block traffic. He put a flashing blue light on the roof of his car. Sergeant Downs and another officer stopped behind him, lights flashing.

"Stay in the car, Peck," Larry said.

Larry got out and walked to the house, motioning for Downs to be ready. It was the fourth time he pressed the doorbell button when he heard gunfire, a shot from inside the house. He turned and pointed at Peck to get down.

"Get behind the car, and get down!" Larry shouted.

Peck opened his door, rolled out and dropped to the ground. Larry flagged Downs to come help.

There was another gunshot inside the house.

Larry called for backup and he and Downs rammed the front door open and rushed in.

A third shot rang out.

On the ground Peck's phone rang. It was Millie.

"Millie, this not a good time."

"I miss you so much. One more test and I'm coming to New Orleans. Will you tell Lily Cup?"

"That's so good, bébé, for true, but I'm unner' a police car and we at this place."

"Peck, I used the number Elizabeth told me about …"

"Hanh?"

"The number that protects people kidnapped, like that little girl."

"Millie, what you talkin about?"

"Was it okay I used it?"

"What number you talkin' about, bébé?"

"Elizabeth was worried, and it scared me."

"Why was Elizabeth worried, bébé?"

"She said you only go to Baton Rouge for readings when you're worried about something, Peck. Then she told me it was okay, and not to worry because you had a phone number to use if there was any trouble, and it would keep you safe, and it would get sex slaves safe."

As Millie spoke, sirens could be heard coming from both directions on the street. Peck turned to look but stayed on the ground as instructed.

"Elizabeth don't know any number, Millie," Peck said. "Nobody give you a number. Lauren, the pedicab girl was there, and she told me Elizabeth didn't give you a number."

"Elizabeth didn't give me the number."

"See, I know that, bébé."

"You gave it to me."

"Hanh!?"

"You texted it to me, remember?"

Peck stood up listening to Millie, while eyeing the door of the mansion like a peregrine falcon.

"Nah-nah, no way, bébé."

"Want me to send you what you texted me?"

"Text me what you think I sent, bébé."

A photo text came to Peck's phone. In it Peck, Gabe and their friend Damas were standing arm and arm, smiling into the camera. It was a picture the saxophone player at Charlie's Blue Note took of Peck, Gabe, and Damas standing by their table, posing. Gabe's arm was around Damas's shoulder, beers were in Damas's and in Peck's hands and a near empty tumbler was in Gabe's hand. Magnified through Gabe's tumbler you could read the black permanent marker phone number scratched on Gabe's palm. It was the phone number Peck had written on Gabe's palm the day he and Gabe visited all the concierges.

"Peck, I sent the number a picture of *The Hanged Man* and said you think he should be hung. Are you mad at me?"

Peck tightened his lips. He knew what it was like to lose a catch. He knew what it was like to turn the wrong way in a bayou. He knew what it was like to have to cut a line, lose a net. He's seen a snapper snatch his bait snake and drop in the water and swim to the bottom with it. His face looked as if he was thinking—*if I could make that mistake what other mistakes did I make?*"

"I love you so much, Millie."

"You told me about the sex slaves, Peck, and I was so worried I went online and found a site selling sex with a young, pregnant girl in New Orleans. It was awful, Peck. A pregnant girl, can you imagine? I was upset and texted the site URL to the phone number on Gabe's hand, and I sent *The Hanged Man* picture and said that's what you would do with that bad man."

Peck winced. He dropped to his knees.

"Are you mad at me, Peck?"

Peck didn't speak. He stared at the pavement and listened to the sirens coming closer.

"That's not all Peck, please don't be mad."

"What else, bébé?"

"I texted a quote from *Deuteronomy* 22:25."

"What quote, bébé?"

'But if in the open country a man meets a young woman who is betrothed, and the man seizes her and lies with her, then only the man who lay with her shall die.'

"Was that a bad thing to do, Peck?"

Peck knew then that Millie caused the hanged man murders. His forehead rested on the side of the police car. His eyes a blank stare as if he had a premonition that his adopted Godfather, André, a parent, would have sensed the message came from him as a wish and that his Millie was only the messenger.

"Promise me to the grave, Millie?"

"To the grave? Don't scare me. What do you mean?"

"Promise you'll never tell anybody you used the number."

"I promise. Did something bad happen?"

Peck didn't respond.

"I promise, Peck. Don't be mad."

"Oh, bébé, Peck is not mad at my Millie."

"I miss you so much, Peck."

"I tell you ever'thing when I see you. I love you Millie, I got to go. Text me when you comin' to New Or-lee-anh."

"I will. I love you Peck, and don't worry. I've already deleted that picture. It's gone."

Three squad cars pulled behind Larry's car on the street. One came from the other direction, and an ambulance drove onto the side lawn of the mansion.

Peck stood up and leaned on the car to watch.

40.

THE MOVIE MOGUL FROM THE HAMPTONS had fired three rounds in his third-floor ballroom after he saw the police cars collecting on the street in front of his house.

"Fuck—piss—shit," he growled. "Robert, who knew about today?"

"Never. Nobody—why do you always—?"

"Because I saw the empty bottles, Robert. Who've you been blabbing your mouth to, you homophilic sot?"

"Fuck you!"

"God damn it, look at the street!"

The movie mogul opened a cabinet and lifted a semiautomatic revolver. The first shot was accidentally discharged, the bullet barely missing his assistant, Robert, but hitting ten-year-old Jewel in the neck, killing her instantly. The preteen sex slave was in a wig and full makeup and wearing a wedding dress. Her body tumbled backward on the floor in a pool of blood, her face pressing the baseboard of the wall.

"You killed her!" Tiffany screamed.

He looked at Tiffany with stone-cold eyes.

"I'll bet this was all your doing, you ungrateful little tart."

He pointed the gun at Tiffany.

"No!" she screamed.

Robert rushed toward him, trying to grab the gun out of his hand. The gun fired, hitting Tiffany in the chest. As Larry and Sergeant Downs could be heard stomping up the stairs, closing in, the movie producer put the gun to his head and pulled the trigger.

Leaning on Larry's car, Peck watched a gurney with a covered body being lifted into the ambulance on the side lawn. Peck was a tracker; a survivor and his gut instincts knew an ambulance ride was at the very minimum a sign that the body on the gurney might still be alive.

Peck didn't learn until later that it was Tiffany being rushed to a hospital for emergency surgery. The movie mogul's personal secretary, Robert, was found in a hidden room filled with equipment, lighting and tapes of child pornography. He was read his rights and arrested.

The four men who were drugged and left on the top steps of Orleans Criminal Court at Tulane and Broad with their foreheads carved agreed to talk, under protection of Larry's promise of anonymity. The numbers on their foreheads were, in fact, their room numbers in different hotels and yes, they had trafficked—purchased sex. Two through different pimps both of them found online. One of them had used the same pimp for five years, a female. The fourth was given a pimp's number by someone at their company's annual sales meeting. That pimp was selling his girlfriend. After having sex, their room phones would ring and a woman's voice would invite them to a pool party, as thanks for being a good customer. A free limo ride to the party was a part of the *thank you.* They were picked up separately and as each stepped into the limo, the driver told them of a Jell-O-shot on the side 'bar' panel but failed to tell them it was laced with Ketamine. Within minutes they would be in a coma.

That evening Larry told Peck where Tiffany was. She had pulled through surgery and was awake but weak and in intensive care. Peck drove to Canal Street and parked. He walked into the French Quarter, looking for Lauren. He saw a row of pedicabs. Lauren was standing by hers, looking at her iPhone. Peck walked over.

"Hey bébé, where you at?"

Lauren looked up and smiled.

"Hi."

"Come hold my hand," Peck said.

"Huh?" Lauren grinned. "What are you up to?"

"I need you to come with me, bébé."

"Now?"

"Lock your pedicab thing and come for something?"

"Where we going, Peck? What's up?"

"It's Tiffany, bébé."

"Is she okay?"

"We found her."

"Hold on!" Lauren shouted.

She pushed her pedicab to a bike stand and chained it. She ran to Peck, took his hand and they hurried to Canal Street and his pickup. Peck started it and pulled away.

"Where was she? Is she okay?" Lauren asked.

"Tiffany's in hospital, bébé. She got shot, but she goin' to be okay, I think."

"What?! Oh no."

"You have to go see her."

As Peck pulled into the hospital, he called Larry.

"Talk to me," Larry said.

"Larry, my pedicab frien'—the one who was with Tiffany when she got beat up by that pimp on Carrollton, can she go up and see Tiffany? We're at the hospital."

"What's her name?"

"Lauren. She's a nice person, Larry, dass for true."

"Tell Lauren to go to the third floor, ask for Detective Grace. Tell Detective Grace that Lieutenant Gaines said she could see Tiffany, and if there's any question have Detective Grace call me."

"Thanks, Larry."

Peck clicked the phone off and looked at Lauren.

"I heard!" Lauren shouted as she jumped from the pickup, closed the door and rushed up steps into the hospital.

Peck turned the engine off. He stared out his window at a sign that read EMERGENCY with a look as if he was reflecting on the day, on his confession, on his life. It was a look as if he realized he was responsible for having caused things to happen because of traps he had set. His look also told that he learned there was a responsibility not to get others in trouble by their innocently trying to help. He labored over the thought he might have to tell Millie what happened as a result of her texting the number. He likely knew he had to find André at Charlie's, and get the phone back.

As Peck sat and thought in his pickup in the parking area, Lauren went into a hospital intensive care unit where Tiffany was in bed, her eyes closed and tubes in her nostrils and one down her throat. Her hair was an expensive auburn and golden ombré, professionally cut short on the sides and pixie on top. Her nose and pouty lips were those of an innocent young teen, one dark freckle to the left of her lower lip. Heavy makeup and liner was on and around her eyes, and her lips smudge-marked as if a hand had wiped across her face. There was no nose ring on her, but a clip-on ring lay on the table next to a large cup of ice water and a straw.

The heart monitor hanging next to her bed was making a constant, comforting *bip, bip, bip.* Tiffany's right hand was taped with a needle in her vein, tubing of saline fluid coming from a plastic bag hanging over the other side of the bed. The fingers of that hand squeezed a gathering of top sheet, as if it were a warm thumb she was holding for comfort. Lauren sat in a chair next to her bed.

"It's me," Lauren whispered.

She took Tiffany's hand.

"It's Lauren," Lauren said.

With both hands she caressed Tiffany's hand and kissed it.

Without opening her eyes Tiffany weakly squeezed Lauren's hand, as if confirming she knew the voice, and it was a welcomed voice.

"You're safe now. Forever. I promise. You're safe."

A tear made its way down Tiffany's mascara. Lauren didn't interrupt its journey into a new life, into a life of reopened hope. She leaned down and kissed Tiffany's hand, then rested on the mattress and looked up.

"I know you've got a real name—so what's your name?—I mean I can't be going around calling you Tiffany to my friends—they'll think we're a couple of hookers—I mean, after all?"

Tiffany's lips attempted a smile.

"Aha, made you laugh," Lauren mumbled.

Tiffany pulled her hand from Lauren's and formed a sign language C with her fingers.

"Is that a c?"

Tiffany gave a weak thumbs up.

"Constance."

No response.

"Charlotte."

No response.

"Carol."

No response.

"Cathy? Cynthia?"

No response.

"Chloe?"

Chloe gave a thumbs up. A tear dropped from her eye.

A nurse stepped in.

"Your friend Tiffany needs to rest now. You'll have to come back," the nurse said.

"This girl is not Tiffany, and she's not my friend."

Chloe's fingers squeezed Lauren's hand.

"Excuse me?" the nurse asked.

"Her name is Chloe. Please correct it on her charts. And Chloe happens to be my sister. Please change that on her records—on that clipboard."

Lauren winked at the nurse, hoping she would play along. She did. She smiled.

"Oh, I am so sorry, I didn't know," the nurse said.

Lauren winked again.

"Nurse, how are Chloe's vital signs, her temp, heart rate, you know, everything?"

"Chloe is going to be fine. She just needs rest."

Lauren leaned over and kissed Chloe on the cheek.

"Bye, sis, I'll come back in the morning."

Chloe squeezed and Lauren kissed her hand, set it on the bed and stepped to the door.

"You like animals, Chloe?"

Chloe did a weak thumbs up.

"Good. You're going to love Oklahoma, our horses and goats. You'll love your house and new family."

Happy tears filled Chloe's eyes.

In the hall Lauren asked the nurse if someone could wash the makeup off Chloe's face.

41.

LILY CUP OPENED THE SIDE DOOR of the shotgun without knocking.

"Anybody home?"

"In the living room—pour a cup," Gabe said.

"Where is everybody?"

Lily Cup came in and sat on the chair beside Gabe.

"Millie got in last night, little sister. Guess where they've been since her eleven p.m. flight?"

"What's it been for them, how many months? My imagination flails with thoughts of what's going on in that room, Gabe—with our 'blue boy' in there."

"At least he'll be calm," Gabe mused.

Gabe and Lily Cup talked about everyone being invited to a special dinner at Commander's Palace as author Simon Dermott's guests and then everyone cabbing over to Charlie's Blue Note, where Charlie promised to have a table waiting, big enough for the whole party. Peck came into the living room, chicory in hand, scratching his abs through a black T-shirt.

"How you all are, cher?"

"You coming out for oxygen son?"

"Is Millie awake?" Lily Cup asked.

"Nah-nah, give her a hour, maybe. Maybe more. She had tests all yesterday and flied here late."

"Good," Lily Cup said. "We need to talk."

"Okay," Peck said.

"And let's keep our voices down," Lily Cup said. "Little children have big ears."

She referred affectionately to Millie. She winked.

The tension of the past week or two were in the eyes of both Gabe and Peck. They had been soldier and tracker on a mission— but they knew the only time Lily Cup ever came to the house unannounced was when Gabe was charged with homicide. They sensed this wasn't a social call. Peck sat on a foot stool, and he and Gabe waited for Lily Cup's lead.

"We're the three musketeers?" Lily Cup asked.

Peck and Gabe nodded, confirming.

"You ever skip a stone on water?" Lily Cup asked.

Peck and Gabe both nodded.

"I could toss a seven-skip stone bounce at Harvard—Lake Cochituate —that's in Boston."

No response.

"I'm going to skip a stone here, maybe a few. You two just nod if you're with me."

Peck and Gabe nodded. They waited.

Lily Cup collected her thoughts.

"We have history," Lily Cup said. "You two and me, we know things. Things that could maybe get me disbarred. Embarrassed at the very least."

Gabe and Peck waited.

"Fishing line ring a bell?" Lily Cup asked. "Black fishing line?"

Peck sat forward.

"No names, Peck—how were they signaled? The room numbers? Not to who, I don't want to know that, just how do the room numbers get signaled?"

"A—how you say—prepaid phone, cher."

"You're telling me a fucking prepaid phone has made all this news in the city? Hell, it's even got the networks talking about the dangers of getting laid in New Orleans."

Peck smiled.

"Somethin' I got to tell you, cher."

Lily Cup waited.

"It's about that phone."

"The prepaid?"

"Ah *oui*, like I say, cher, prepaid phone ..."

Lily Cup sipped her chicory, waiting.

"Not me, but somebody told Millie the number and told her it was a magic number to save sex-slaved girls and she saw on her computer a pregnant girl bein' sold in New Or-lee-anh—"

"Don't tell me—" Lily Cup started.

Peck was silent.

"—and she texted it to the number," Lily Cup said.

"Ah *oui*. Millie don't know what happened, cher."

"Don't tell her."

"Okay."

"But if she finds out, will she keep it buttoned?" Lily Cup asked.

"Forever, cher, I promise."

"Time to put a stop to this, guys," Lily Cup said. "I don't know how you did it, but the girl is free, and that was the mission. It's over, both of you."

Both Gabe and Peck nodded.

"Get me the phone, Peck. It's over."

"Okay."

"Don't stop its signals, just get me the phone."

"Okay."

"Wipe it clean of prints, but don't break it."

"Okay."

"Here's the deal, guys. I'm seeing Larry."

"Seeing Larry? Like …?" Gabe started.

"I got in a bathtub with him. Use your imagination."

"My brother, a good man, little sister," Gabe said.

"My generation had less racial hang-ups than the previous generations. I had a crush on him in high school. He was a basketball star. We never connected. I went to Harvard after graduation and he went his way."

"Larry is a good guy, dass for true," Peck said.

"I think I'm falling in love with him."

Peck and Gabe smiled.

"He told me about your 'talk,' Peck. How you did it. That was smart, you letting him hear. He trusts you to help do investigative work. That's a big deal. He likes you and sees you maybe becoming a detective someday."

"With—how you say—what I done, cher. How could I?"

Lily Cup held up her hand.

"Musketeer secret time."

Both Gabe and Peck raised their hands swearing to a Musketeer secret.

"Gabe, leave the room," Lily Cup said.

The military in Gabe didn't let him think twice. He stood and went to his bedroom and pulled the door closed.

Lily Cup whispered: "Does Gabe know about the two you—?"

"Nah, nah. Nobody know but the priest and Larry."

Lily Cup leaned in. "And me," Lily Cup added.

"Ah *oui*."

"Coroner O'Sullivan is a friend of mine. We went to grade school together."

"Ah *oui*?"

"The top sheet on his case file for the dead Porsche guy now reads he was run into, his forehead hit the steering wheel, killed him instantly. The top sheet on the case file for pimp man now says he tripped on a wet sidewalk in the rain, fatally hitting his head on a concrete stair. His forehead and head were bruised."

"Oh, cher, does Larry—?"

"No one knows, Peck. Only you and me."

"The coroner, cher?"

"You are such a tracker, Peck. You are amazing."

"Well, cher, does he?"

"Let's just say the coroner and I finished up some business we started in the fourth grade. He turned a blind eye, and his lips are sealed."

Peck took Lily Cup's hand and kissed it.

"I like Larry a lot, dass for true, but after Tulane I'm thinkin' me and Millie have crawfish and chickens some place. Three acres, cher."

"Time will tell. Finish up at Tulane."

"Cher, can I give you something for Larry?"

"Of course."

Peck took a SIM card from his pocket.

"This is from that dollar tattoo pimp's phone, cher."

Lily Cup leaned in and kissed Peck on the forehead.

"Gabe," Lily Cup shouted. "You can come in."

Gabe came in, carrying a coffee pot to fill mugs.

"Are we proud of my brother, little sister?" Gabe asked.

"We really are," Lily Cup said. "Dass for true," she joked.

"What will you do with the phone, cher?"

"I'm giving it and this SIM card to Larry. Think of the hero he's going to be with vice."

"Perfect," Gabe said.

"Peck, however that phone gets the room numbers sent to it, don't stop it. Keep it going—but don't be involved in any way."

Lily Cup finished her coffee, stood and started for the kitchen.

"See you guys tonight at Commander's Palace?" Lily Cup asked.

"We wouldn't miss it," Gabe said. "Tuxedoes?"

"Why not?" Lily Cup said. "Suit and ties will work too, but tell Miss Millie to pull out that Chanel and the French stockings, cause we're partying with an author and some other bigwigs, and Lady Sasha will be inspecting shoes and sacred haute at the door."

With grins shared she left through the side door.

42.

A FULL MOON lit parts of Washington Avenue not shaded by the live oak of New Orleans. Men in suits and ties accompanied dressy companions and lined out the door at Commander's Palace, a hint that every table inside was full and plated with a nouvelle Creole cuisine that has been topic of food conversations worldwide since the early days of *joie de vivre.*

In a reserved private room, author Simon Dermott stood at the head of the table, a goblet of Chateau Lafite Rothschild in his hand. His wife, Nicole, was seated along with guests around the table, including Sasha, Gabe, Lily Cup, Lieutenant Gaines (Larry), Damas, Peck, and Millie.

A broad, blue satin ribbon stretched the length of the table diagonally. The ribbon was a fabled Commander's Palace award of recognition.

Simon raised his glass in toast.

"Thank you all for coming. Nicole and I are honored. We're blessed to have good friends in New Orleans, being welcomed into your households, your court and your culture. Damas, my friend and talented, inquisitive, and steadfast researcher of all things Acadiana has shared rich, bountiful stories and secrets he's learned from you who have been gracious enough to share them; insights on topics for a novel I've been sweating bullets over for—Wednesday it will be a year."

"Here, here," Lieutenant Gaines said.

"I understand," Simon started, "that following our dining in this national treasure, this monument to good taste, a table surrounded by sounds of jazz awaits near Frenchman Street—and '*If music be the food of love,* those of you willing and able shall *play on.*"

Simon sat to polite applause.

Lieutenant Larry Gaines stood.

"So long as we're on the 'Bard,' may I lift my glass to a friend, a colleague fondly known to most as *Peck*. Mr. Boudreaux Clemont Finch, here's to you, my friend: *'Some are born great, some achieve greatness, and some have greatness thrust upon them.'* My friend, you are all of the above."

"Speech, speech, speech!" Gabe, Sasha, Lily Cup, Damas, and Millie called out in unison.

Peck, with his face a red blush, stood.

Tears glistened in his eyes as he looked at Gabe, at Millie, at Sasha, and at Lily Cup.

"Mémé was pregnant with my mamma when she saw her family get drowned in Bayou Chene by the Mississippi River mud and silt. In lightnin' and rain my pregnant mémé walked herself barefoot forty miles to Mandeville, where she come to the edge of Lake Ponchartrain. Mémé was cold and wet from the rain, and hungry I bet, dass for true. My mamma told me that when Mémé looked up to the heavens for an answer where to go an airplane flew over, an Eastern Airlines jet exploded in the sky and it fell into Lake Ponchartrain and sunk to the bottom. Mémé saw a doll floating and a little girl's coat floating. Dass when Mémé went to an insane place, where my mamma got born. My mamma and some others at that insane place got raped and then I was born. So why am I telling you this? When I'm not reading a book or when I'm trying to get smarter at Tulane in night school, I clean offices. Cleaning Lily Cup's office, I saw out the window a man on Carrollton hitting a girl—a twelve-year-old girl, and stealing her away to sell for sex. I call him a man, but he's not a man. He's a worm, he's a fire ant, he's a pimp. That bad man called that little girl Tiffany. But that isn't her name—her name is Chloe.

"Ladies and gentlemen,—Chloe is free tonight. No more slave for sex. Chloe is at the hospital with my frien' who helped me find her, Lauren. Lauren would be here, but she staying with Chloe, helping her get better."

Peck sat. He stared down at the plate in front of him. Not a sound at a table while guests reflected on his words.

Two hands slowly clapped. It was Larry. Then Gabe began to clap. Millie. Lily Cup and Sasha. All joined in to warm, heartfelt appreciation that touched everyone's heart.

THE END

HISTORICAL FICTION books by ANTIL
(*Pompey Hollow Book Club* series)

THE MYSTERIES OF POMPEY HOLLOW - 1949
*(2*nd *Edition of THE POMPEY HOLLOW BOOK CLUB)*

THE DELPHI FALLS TRILOGY - 1953

SUMMER OF SHADOWS, BODIES & BRIDGES - 1953
*(2*nd *Edition of THE BOOK OF CHARLIE – Spirit of the Pompey Hollow Book Club)*

SIDESHOW PICKPOCKET - 1953
*(The 2*nd *Edition of MARY CRANE – Séance with Sherlock)*

HEAVEN SENDS FOR HEMINGWAY - 1953
*(The 2*nd *Edition of HEMINGWAY, THREE ANGELS, and ME)*

AUTOBIOGRAPHICAL books by ANTIL

THE LONG STEM IS IN THE LOBBY - '58 to '61
From Bad Times to Good Times - How I found My Way

HOME ON THE RANGE – 1902 - 2021

SUSPENSE/MYSTERY books by ANTIL

ONE MORE LAST DANCE

THE HOODOO OF PECK FINCH
Sequel to One More Last Dance

MAMMA'S MOON - Duet Novel
(One More Last Dance & The Hoodoo of Peck Finch)

SELF HELP book by ANTIL

HANDBOOK FOR WEEKEND DADS…and Anytime grandparents.)

www.ingramcontent.com/pod-product-compliance
Lightning Source LLC
Chambersburg PA
CBHW021322190726

48288CB00003B/921